S0-BBB-436

Tiger Butte

Also by Jack Cummings
in Thorndike Large Print ®

Deserter Troop
Escape From Yuma
Rebels West!
The Surrogate Gun

This Large Print Book carries the
Seal of Approval of N.A.V.H.

Tiger Butte

Jack Cummings

Thorndike Press • Thorndike, Maine

Library of Congress Cataloging in Publication Data:

Cummings, Jack, 1925-
    Tiger Butte / Jack Cummings.
        p.   cm.
    ISBN 1-56054-439-2 (alk. paper : lg. print)
    1. Large type books.   I. Title.
[PS3553.U444T5   1993]   92-36426
813'.54—dc20   CIP

All the characters and events portrayed in this story are
fictitious.

Thorndike Large Print® Western Series edition published
in 1993 by arrangement with Walker & Company, Inc.

Cover design by Ron Walotsky.

The tree indicium is a trademark of Thorndike Press.

This book is printed on acid-free, high opacity paper. ∞

Author's Note

In the 1870s the wealth of the silver mines of Southern California's Mojave Desert lured the *californio* bandits across the Sierras from the central valleys. The most notorious of these badmen was the historical, legendary Tiburcio Vásquez, but he was caught and hanged.

Another, who is fictitious, was Sabás Orozco, and he too hated the *yanquis* for what he thought they had done to his people.

The richest silver mines of the desert were on a barren mountain called by the Mexicans *Cerro Gordo*, which means Fat Hill. The *Sierra Gorda* of this novel is fictitious.

But Tiger Butte, known now by a different name, is there as it was when Orozco and Belle Jackson met their respective fates.

PROLOGUE

The Bodie Kid was thirty feet away when he threw down on John Leslie with a brand new Colt Peacemaker.

The Bodie kid was eighteen when he died. His career as a gunfighter lasted less than an hour. It began at noon on April 17, 1878, and ended fifty-five minutes later on the crooked main street of the silver-mining town of Jericho, Arizona Territory, where John Leslie had been the marshal for ten years.

In that fifty-five minutes the Bodie Kid, who was really a young saddle tramp named Bert Sutter, had bought his new gun and holster in Janofsky's hardware store, got drunk in the Fatima Saloon, boasted of his fighting prowess, walked unsteadily out into the sunlight to prove it, and got himself killed.

He also managed, with a drunk's luck, to put two bullets into the marshal, one in his right thigh and one in his left buttock as the first bullet turned Leslie around.

John Leslie had been taken by surprise, which he wouldn't have been five years before. That was half of it. The other half was just as bad or worse — his reflexes had failed him. He was slow getting his gun out, and he had gutshot the Kid while shooting for his arm.

John Leslie sat in a wheelchair in the cemetery as they dropped the Kid into his grave and stuck a wooden marker over it.

Staring at the epitaph on the marker, he kept seeing it worded differently. He kept seeing how close he'd come to having it read:

JOHN LESLIE
Lawman
Born 1838 — Died 1878

And I never really had a woman of my own, he thought.

He thought then of Belle, who a whiskey drummer from the Coast, knowing Leslie and Belle had once been somewhat taken with each other, had told him was now a widow and running a boardinghouse out Los Angeles way.

John Leslie had close to a thousand dollars saved, which wasn't much for risking his life every day for ten years, and that helped to make his decision. That, and being so close to being killed by the likes of the Bodie Kid.

As soon as his wounds healed, he drew his money out of the bank, quit his job, and took the stage west to Yuma, where the Southern Pacific had now reached with its tracks from California.

Two weeks later a stranger rode into Jericho, a lean man, nearing thirty, with strong, tanned features and sun-squint creases around his eyes.

He wore range clothes mostly, but his boots were cavalry, and covering his shock of black hair was a battered campaign hat. There was a Colt .45 slung at his side and a Winchester '73 carbine in his saddle scabbard, and he looked capable of using either.

He was newly resigned from the army's employ where he had been for eight years a civilian scout for the cavalry against the Apaches.

He too was headed west, having in mind to somehow make himself a stake in California that would enable him to settle down. His name was Tom Sutter, and he had detoured by Jericho to see his kid brother, Bert, who had been working recently, he'd heard, in the vicinity.

What he learned in Jericho did not change his direction, but it changed his intentions.

CHAPTER 1

The train pulled into the pueblo of Los Angeles, which now had a population of eight thousand. John Leslie wondered if she remembered how it was between them? Ten years is a hell of a long time. Especially in the life of a law dog now reached forty. Belle, she'd be close to thirty now, he guessed. Would her looks be gone? Somehow he couldn't, or wouldn't, believe that.

Well, he'd soon know. God, he'd wanted her, back there when she was slinging hash in Jericho. And her saying, "No, John. I can't live through every day afraid I'll be a widow."

And him, as a newly hired marshal, after kicking around loose following three years in the Union army, saying, "I can't give up what I am to be a store clerk, Belle. Or go back to being a ranch hand at twenty-five a month. What the hell else can I make a decent living at?"

"Then I'm sorry, John Leslie," she had said. She only called him by his full name when she was mad.

Then a few months later, Fred Jackson, a young miner working a claim of his own, had struck it moderately lucky and sold out and announced he was heading for the Coast. He had personality and good looks, Fred did, and when he'd offered to marry Belle and take her with him, she'd accepted.

And she had ended up a widow anyway, Leslie thought. But he took no satisfaction in that. Not if it had brought her grief. He'd never want to see Belle grieving. Not ever. His feeling for her was too strong.

He'd expected all the structures in the town to be adobes, but only the older ones were, the ones built when the Mexicans owned the place. Now there were wood frame houses and stores scattered around. *Yanqui* buildings were taking over, some even of kilned brick.

He pulled out the slip of paper with the address the drummer had given him, just to make sure he had it right. He'd already found the street.

It wasn't a big place, but he figured it could have six or so rooms for rent, plus the kitchen and a parlor. There was a Room and Board sign hung on the wood post of a wide, roofed veranda.

He climbed up the steps, his recent wounds still giving him a twinge. He set down his battered valise and knocked on the door.

She hasn't changed, he thought gratefully. Her figure was still slim. Her face was matured, as it should be, but still attractive as ever. Her light brown hair showed no gray. Her brown eyes met his frankly as she appraised him.

"I'm looking for lodging, ma'am," he said. It was hard to keep his voice casual.

Then he saw the recognition come.

"Johnny! Oh God!" And she was in his arms, clinging to him.

It had been a long time since he had held her like that. He wanted to hold her like that forever.

They sat in the parlor, the two of them alone, and he said, "What happened to Fred?"

Her eyes studied his face as she answered. "His heart stopped. He'd been working as a freighter, hoping to clear the mortgage we owe the bank on this place. He keeled over dead one day with a fourteen-mule-team jerkline in his hands. Out on the Mojave Desert."

"I'm sorry," he said. "Freighting what?"

"Silver ingots down from the mines at Sierra Gorda. He worked for Remi Nadeau." She paused. "Remi Nadeau had a hauling contract for all the Inyo mines. At times he had fifty teams strung out across the desert, each drawing three wagons. On the return trips they took back supplies."

"That many?"

"Silver's made this town grow in recent years. It's made the farmers and the gringo cattle raisers prosper, supplying grain to Nadeau, food for the mining camps."

"Gringos? What about the old Mexican dons?"

"Almost all of them lost out to the sharp business methods of the *yanquis* years ago."

"Yeah. I heard something about that," Leslie said. "This Sierra Gorda, where is that?"

"Two hundred and twenty miles from here, north across the desert. In the Inyo range close to Death Valley. It was a twenty-two-day round-trip for a freighter. Now they only freight from the mines down to the railhead town of Mojave. Once the Southern Pacific reached there they began shipping direct up to San Francisco."

He said now, "Belle, your years with Fred — were they good ones?"

She hesitated, then said, "They were good enough, John."

"When did it happen?"

"It has been three years now."

There was a silence between them, and then he said, "Belle, I want you to know I intend to hang up my guns."

She did not show the enthusiasm he had expected.

"I thought you'd be pleased. It was what you once wanted."

"Yes. Yes, I remember I did."

"And now?"

"What will you do?"

"I'm not broke. I have a few hundred dollars."

She nodded.

"I'll find something."

"Yes. Yes, of course."

"I mean I have plenty enough to pay my room and board."

"John! You know I wasn't thinking of that."

"I wanted you to know." He hesitated. "You said you have a mortgage to pay on this place. I don't mean to pry, Belle. But can I help in any way?"

She gave him a speculative look but said nothing.

"Tell me."

She said finally, her voice low and embarrassed. "The note at the bank — it's overdue. They're going to foreclose."

"How much?"

"Three thousand dollars."

He was stunned.

"We'd have made it if Fred hadn't died. But since then — well, the bank has refused me any more extensions."

He said, "If I went to them and paid up some interest —"

"I couldn't let you. Anyway, it would just be throwing good money after bad to gain a little time. Where would I ever get all those thousands of dollars?"

The day following his arrival he rented a horse and buggy at the Bear State Livery nearby, and they went for a drive out eastward into the San Gabriel valley toward the mission. It was a bright, sunlit morning, the San Gabriel Mountains looming high to the north, the graze-covered ranges of hills to the south still green from the spring rains.

She said, "Sometimes I think of how this must have been when the dons ran their thousands of cattle here. They lived an idyllic life until the *yanquis* came. Is it any wonder that Mexican resentment is everywhere?"

"Maybe not," he said. "Still, what they had was too good to last. They should have known that."

"Why? They could have gone on forever if the Americans hadn't come."

"Maybe. But what's done is done. You can never go back."

She took his arm and pressed it tightly. "*We* can, John," she said. "*We* can. Do you want to?"

They went back to the house and made love in her room.

"God!" she said, "I have waited a long time for this."

He was silent, holding her to him as if she might get away. All the wasted years, he thought. All the wasted life.

"I should have married you," she said. "I never should have made you choose between me and your job."

"I understand, Belle. You wanted security."

"And I ended up without it after all."

"You were right, though," he said. He was thinking back to how close the Bodie Kid had come to killing him.

"No, I was wrong. I should have known you were too good with a gun to get killed."

He shook his head. "No. Nobody is ever that good." He had told her about his shoot-out with the Kid. "That's why I quit. That last time it was too close."

She drew away slightly to study his face. "You haven't lost your nerve, Johnny?"

He did not answer at once. "Is it important?"

"Isn't it to you?"

He lay silent and stared at the ceiling.

"Isn't it?" she said.

"Yeah, I guess it is. I was hoping it wouldn't be."

"Well then," she said.

"Well then, what?"

"Don't hang up your gun on my account. In spite of all the risks you've taken, you've outlived Fred."

"Why not? I'll find something else to do."

"What? Like you once asked me — clerk in a store? Be a ranch hand? There's no money in that out here either."

"Is money that important?"

She thought before she answered. "I worked and Fred worked to get what I've got — this house. Now they're going to take it from me. That makes me think that money is important."

"I said I'd help you."

"It's not your problem."

"I'll make it mine."

"No. That wouldn't be right. I wouldn't feel right about that, Johnny."

"It would be my decision."

"I couldn't," she said. Then abruptly she began to make love to him again.

Much later she said, "With your reputation, you could get on as a sheriff's deputy."

He did not reply.

"You wouldn't want that?"

He said, "Belle, I want to help you. I'd never be able to do it on a deputy's pay."

He paused. "There's more to it than that though."

"Your nerve?"

Irritated, he said, "Why do you keep asking that?"

"I'm sorry."

"What I meant was something different. If I could just figure some way to make a good stake, something to pay off the bank for you."

She got up from the bed. She crossed to the dresser, saying, "I didn't know whether to mention this to you or not." She picked up a folded copy of the *Los Angeles Star* of the day before and brought it to him. She pointed to a news story on the front page:

GOVERNOR INCREASES REWARD FOR OROZCO CAPTURE
Proclamation of Above:
State of California
Executive Department
Sacramento, California
June 20, 1878

Whereas, in recent months in the southern counties of California, several robberies and killings have been perpetrated by one Sabás Orozco; and, not withstanding an earlier proclamation offering a substantial reward for his apprehension, he is still at large and is engaged in violating the laws and committing crimes in the southern part of the state. Now, therefore, revoking the former proclamation of a $1,000 reward previously issued, by the authority in me vested, and in pursuance of a special law enacted for the purpose of arresting and punishing such criminals, I, Layton Birch, governor of the State of California, do hereby offer a reward of $3,000 for the arrest of the said Sabás Orozco, payable on his being delivered alive to the sheriff of the county of Los Angeles; and I do further proclaim that if during an attempt to arrest him he shall make such resistance as to endanger the persons or the lives of whosoever may arrest him, and shall in consequence thereof be killed, I offer a reward of $2,000, payable upon proof of his death and the circumstances attending it, to the man or men who may have killed him. Only one of the above rewards will be paid. If Sabás Orozco shall necessarily be killed, the said sum of $2,000 will be paid; if he be arrested and delivered to the sheriff of Los Angeles County alive, the sum of $3,000 will be paid.

Layton Birch, Governor

"I have never been a bounty hunter," John Leslie said.

"Three thousand dollars, John."

He was thoughtful. "It would pay off the bank."

"I wasn't thinking of that. Really."

"Tell me something about this Orozco. He's Mexican by his name," Leslie said.

"A black sheep son of an old *californio* family, some say. He once rode with Tiburcio Vásquez."

"Hung him, didn't they? Vásquez, I mean."

"Three years back. Vásquez often had confederates. Orozco was a youth embittered by his family's loss of their rancho to the gringos, so the story goes, when he joined him. Since Vásquez was caught, he has ridden alone. The Lone Coyote of the Mojave, they call him. He preys on the silver and payroll shipments of the gringo mine operators in the Inyos and the Panamints. His way of hitting back, I guess."

"You sound like you sympathize with him."

"Perhaps a little. I have come to realize how the *californios* feel, losing all through foreclosures and such. Orozco is something of a folk hero to them."

"But you suggest that I try to hunt him down."

"Not if you don't want to. I just thought

you might be interested."

"It would take care of what you owe," he said.

"Please don't say it like that. It makes me sound like I'm begging."

"Are you?"

She started to deny it, then stopped. For a long time she did not answer. Then she sighed and said, "Maybe I am, Johnny. If I am, I detest myself for it. But it would give us something to live on together. It would be yours too. You do want me with you, don't you, Johnny?"

"You know the answer to that."

"Maybe I shouldn't have showed you that newspaper."

"No," he said. "I'm glad you did. It's worth a try. It's a lot of money, if I can pull it off."

"I wouldn't want anything to happen to you," she said.

"Dammit! Belle, I've got to try."

"Because of me, Johnny?"

"Because of me. You keep asking about my nerve. Maybe I did lose it for a while. Maybe I ran away from Jericho, figuring my string had run out. Now I've been having different thoughts, and I'm bothered by it. You know, a man who lives by his gun — well, it's his pride that keeps him going. I lost something when I quit, I know that now. Maybe this will give it back to me."

"If anything happened to you," she said, "I could never forgive myself."

He ignored this and said, "The Mojave, is it rough country, Belle?"

"Fifteen thousand square miles of burning, sometimes freezing, desert. With scorched mountains that fringe Death Valley itself. That's why no posse has ever caught Orozco out there. No bunch of sworn-in civilians ever has the stamina to keep on this trail. They never caught Vásquez out there either — they caught him when he came here to town."

"If I turn bounty hunter," Leslie said, "where would I start?"

"You'd need a base to operate from," Belle said. "I think perhaps Sierra Gorda would be the place."

CHAPTER 2

Belle had barely put out the Vacancy sign when the tall stranger came up and made inquiry. He was a man of ruggedly handsome features and a smile that showed his appreciation of her looks.

She liked that about him, of course, but she sensed somehow that he was a man to watch out for. There was a hard look of dedication in his amber eyes, an aura of purpose about him that his smile did not hide.

But he was clean and polite enough and had the money she asked for in advance, and she quickly rented John Leslie's room to him.

"Will you be staying long?" she said.

"All depends, ma'am. By the way, the name is Benteen. Tom Benteen."

"I am Belle."

"My pleasure, ma'am."

"I serve supper at seven. I have at present four other boarders. A railroad man, a mining stock trader, a young lady schoolteacher, and an older woman, a seamstress."

"I came by an hour ago and there was no Vacancy sign out."

"I was holding a room for a special guest,

one who recently moved out. I wasn't certain he wouldn't be back."

"And now you are sure? My good luck then. I'm just in from Arizona, and a stranger to Los Angeles." His eyes studied her face as he told her this.

It was his eyes that bothered her, the way they probed for answers. Benteen. The name meant nothing to her.

"Heard there was considerable silver mining hereabouts," he said.

"Yes, Mr. Benteen. There's a silver boom up on the north fringe of the desert backcountry. Second only to Nevada's Comstock, some say."

"A man from a mining town in the Territory, he'd likely look for work there then, wouldn't you say?"

"Yes, of course. But, if you'll pardon my saying so, you do not look like a mining man." Her glance swept from the hat he was holding to his cavalry boots.

His smile widened. "You are observant, ma'am. Matter of fact, army scouting is more in my line."

"Not much call for your profession out here, Mr. Benteen. There's been no real trouble with the southern Paiutes for years. Nor the Shoshones. The army does keep a handful of troopers up at Fort Independence, north of the mines, though. Just in case."

"You seem to be well-informed, ma'am."

"My late husband freighted bullion down from the area regularly. I learned much about it from him."

"You are a mighty pretty widow, Belle."

"I do not encourage familiarity with my guests, Mr. Benteen."

"Of course. I meant no offense by the compliment." He paused, then said, "Do you get many men coming through from the mining towns of Arizona?"

"Not often. Those on the way to the desert mines would likely stay over at the Pico House or some other hotel. A boardinghouse is hardly the place for transient guests. I might add that I'm surprised you sought out my place here."

"I had a reason, ma'am."

"And what would that be?"

"It was recommended to me."

"Oh? By who, Mr. Benteen?"

"Fellow I run into in a town called Jericho, over in the Territory."

She was suddenly frightened.

"He said you used to live there."

She could not deny it. "Yes. Yes, I left ten years ago."

"So I heard. I also heard you used to be some took by the marshal there."

"I do not think that is any business of

yours, Mr. Benteen."

"The word there was that he decided to look you up again, him learning you was now a widow and all." ⸱

"I — I haven't seen him, Mr. Benteen."

"Strange, wouldn't you say? Seeing as he left Jericho a couple of weeks before I did."

"I wouldn't know about that."

"His name was Leslie. You know that, of course. John Leslie. Had somewhat of a reputation as a gunhand."

"Why do you tell me this?"

"Just trying to jog your memory some. You sure he didn't come here, ma'am?"

She never could carry off a lie, and his now-faint smile chilled her. But she said, "No."

"Well, I reckon he'll be along sooner or later. Don't rightly know what would detain him. Was me in his boots, I'd not have wasted time getting here. No offense meant this time either, ma'am. It's another compliment."

"Why do you want to see him?"

"Did I say I did? No, ma'am, I just mentioned him in passing. You asked why I sought out your place here. Well, I learned about it from those people back in Jericho who said he'd come here. I figured that was good enough recommendation."

They were in his room now, the room John Leslie had so recently vacated. He set his battered tan valise on the single chair. "Now, if you don't mind, I'll just rest up a while before the call to supper."

Her eyes stayed on the valise as she said, "Yes, of course. I'll call you a little before time, Mr. Benteen." She went out and closed the door behind her, and for a moment she leaned against it. She heard him moving about behind her, and she started up in panic, then headed toward the kitchen. The initials stamped in black on the valise were T.S., and they did not stand for Tom Benteen. Of that she was certain.

Was he following John for a reason? She could not rid herself of the feeling that he was.

Leslie had mentioned nothing in his past that would account for his being followed from the Territory. In fact he had spoken of nothing except the incident with the Bodie Kid.

"The poor damn young fool," John had said. "He threw away his life trying to prove he was something he wasn't. Makes me sick to think I had to kill him. Shows what rotgut likker can cause a man to do. What I heard, he'd never been in any real trouble before. Just got drunk and started acting crazy and there wasn't nothing else I could do, and I got to live with it on my conscience for the rest of my life."

Belle had said, "His calling himself the Bodie Kid — it seems he wanted to acquire a reputation as a badman."

Leslie shook his head. "Hell, he only called himself that the day I killed him. Thought it up while he was standing at the bar showing off his new gun and holster. Was only a fair-to-middling ranch hand riding the grub line most of the time. His real name was Bert Sutter."

Belle started. *Sutter*. T.S., those initials. Tom Sutter?

She smelled something burning and frantically jerked open the oven door.

Nobody complained about her meal. They were too interested in the new guest. Especially the two women. To them he was a romantic figure. The kind of real-life model about which scores of dime novels were being currently written.

"Did you know Wild Bill Hickok, Mr. Benteen?" Miss Hanna, the schoolteacher said. She was a plain-faced girl, but there was a vibrancy about her that was unexpected in one of her calling.

Mr. Benteen was aware of this at once and seemed willing to take advantage of it. "I'm sorry, I can't say that I did, ma'am. Was he one of your heroes?"

She colored slightly. "Well, of course I do not read trashy novels, Mr. Benteen. But from the news stories about him before his demise — well, I must admit to a certain fascination with his adventurous life. And with yours too, I would imagine."

"Well, I have had some adventures, Miss Hanna."

"Against Indians, Mr. Benteen?"

"Yes, ma'am. Against the Apaches in Arizona."

"Interesting," the railroad man said. "Mighty interesting, I'd reckon."

The mining stock salesman was silent, his attention seeming devoted to his food.

The older woman, a Mrs. Fulton, who retained some signs of an earlier comeliness, said, "My late husband was a cavalry officer, Mr. Benteen."

"In the Territories, ma'am?"

"No. He was killed at Brice's Crossroads. Fighting for Bedford Forrest."

"You have reason to be proud, ma'am."

"Were you in the War, Mr. Benteen?"

"For only the last year, ma'am. I was seventeen at the time."

"And on which side did you fight?"

"It happens I was with the Union."

"I see."

"I hope you don't hold that against me."

"No, Mr. Benteen. There were many widows on either side."

The stock salesman looked up and stared at her. "I never heard you say that before," he said.

Benteen turned his attention back to the schoolmarm. "You ever been in Arizona, Miss Hanna?"

"No. I am a native here."

"In California? You have Spanish blood?"

She laughed. "Mr. Benteen, the gringos have been coming into California for generations. It just took a while for them to gain complete control. My father and mother came here in the mid-fifties. From New England. They recently went back."

"I understand there's bad feelings with the Spanish."

"Spanish? Why do Americans insist on referring to Mexicans as Spanish? Do you know why? Prejudice, Mr. Benteen."

"Prejudice?"

"Indeed. If they did not look down on the Mexicans and the Mexican *californios,* they'd realize these people are proud to be Mexican. But no, the Yankee merchants, with hypocritical courtesy born of their desire to sell goods to the *latinos,* look upon the word 'Mexican' as an epithet and use 'Spanish' as a euphemism. Most Mexicans hate this — they fought a revolution to free themselves from the Spanish."

"I never thought about it that way, ma'am," Benteen said. "I can see now why you are a schoolteacher."

"I didn't mean to sound like one," Miss Hanna said. She smiled. "But tell me, why did you leave Arizona to come here? I mean, did you tire of scouting?"

"Well, I reckon that had something to do with it, at least in the beginning." He glanced covertly at Belle, then back at Miss Hanna. "There's more to it than that now. I have some business to attend to out here."

"Will you be going back when your business is attended to, Mr. Benteen?" Miss Hanna said. "Your life seems so exciting."

"Hard to say," he said. "The excitement comes in spurts."

"Perhaps you can find excitement here in California, Mr. Benteen."

He gave her a studied look. "Yes — maybe I can." He smiled. "Any suggestions?"

She colored. "Hardly. I'm afraid a schoolteacher is hardly knowledgeable about such things."

"Come now. You must be well up on local history. My understanding is that Los Angeles is hardly a quiet place."

"Well, of course we are still a frontier town,

Mr. Benteen. Far behind San Francisco in progress. So we have our share of violence. There is much tension between the Americans and the Mexican *californios* here. But it seldom breaks out into actual confrontations. You can feel it though. You could feel it quite strongly when Tiburcio Vásquez was running rampant in the area. But he has been hanged, going on three years now. Of course there is Orozco, once his protégé, who is making news from time to time."

Benteen was thoughtful. "Is there a reward out on him?"

"Yes. Matter of fact, there is. It has just been increased, I believe." Miss Hanna looked searchingly at him. "Why do you ask?"

"I'm always interested in money, ma'am. Scouting for the army doesn't pay well, and a man should think of his future."

"There, then, is an adventure for you," she said.

"You've given me something to think about."

"It is said that Orozco is on the desert again. A dangerous place, Mr. Benteen. And a dangerous man." Miss Hanna seemed to be titillated by the thought. "He is a rather romantic figure though," she said. She caught his quick stare and blushed.

"I have met some outlaws," Benteen said.

"But I've never heard one described as romantic before."

"You are not a woman," Miss Hanna said. "Did you know that when Vásquez was held here in the jail, women baked pies and cookies and sent them to him?"

"I suppose some Mexican women would sympathize with him," Benteen said.

"I am speaking of white women as well."

Benteen held her eyes with his own. "And were you one of those women, ma'am?"

She blushed and did not answer.

"Were you?"

"Yes. As a matter of truth, I was. You see, Mr. Benteen, I am an incurable romantic."

"I'll remember that, ma'am."

Belle had just come back from the kitchen to serve dessert. She said, "All women are romantic, Mr. Benteen."

"I reckon there's no harm in that," he said. "I am curious though. Did either of you women witness his hanging?"

"Thank the Lord, they took him north to San Jose for that," Miss Hanna said. "I don't think I could have stood it, had it taken place here."

"Sounds like you were an admirer of his, ma'am."

"Of course I wasn't!" She paused. "But he died so bravely, they said. He did not flinch, not even when they placed the noose around his neck."

Belle said, "You must remember, dear, that brave or not, he was a robber who killed several men during the commission of his crimes. Not the sort of man you or I would want to take up with."

Miss Hanna looked at Benteen. She did not reply.

Benteen got the feeling that Miss Hanna might not be entirely in accord with Belle's statement. He toyed briefly with the thought. If he had the time, he might well work some on the young schoolmarm. Her life had to be a dull one. He knew from experience that too much boredom could drive some women to dalliance. If they were tempted.

Mrs. Fulton entered the conversation again. "The brave die young," she said to no one in particular. There was a faraway look in her eyes.

"Were you one who sent gifts to the jail, ma'am?" Benteen said teasingly.

"I was thinking of my long-deceased husband," the widow said. "All those years, Mr. Benteen, without him. All those long, dismal years."

"It surprises me that you didn't marry again, ma'am."

"When I said he died young, I did not mean *that* young. He was a captain. He was past thirty. And I was not much younger. A widow that age finds it hard to get a husband."

The mining stock salesman said, "Had I met you then, Edna, things might have been different. You must have been a very handsome woman."

"That's very gallant of you," Mrs. Fulton said. "And what are your feelings now?"

He looked startled by her bluntness. "Well — I'm past the age for marrying, Edna. A confirmed bachelor. I've told you that before."

Mrs. Fulton flushed. She got up from the table and fled toward her room.

There was a moment of silence.

"How *un*gallant!" Belle said.

The mining stock salesman looked up from his plate. "What did I say wrong?"

Nobody answered him.

Benteen turned to Belle. "And you, ma'am, did you bake for that Mexican bandit?"

"No, I did not, Mr. Benteen."

"You weren't one of those who sympathized with him then?"

"I was married at the time," Belle said. "My husband was still alive."

"And if he hadn't been, would that have made a difference?"

"Your questions are very impertinent, Mr. Benteen."

"Sorry, ma'am. You're right, of course. I'm

just making conversation. It isn't often that I sit at a table with ladies." He smiled, then turned his smile again on Miss Hanna.

She smiled back.

If only I had the time, Benteen thought. If only I didn't have to get that bastard, John Leslie.

The more Belle thought about Benteen, the more certain she was that her suspicions were correct. He *is* Sutter, she told herself. And he's out to get revenge for the killing of his brother.

She had to warn Johnny.

She wondered how a man must feel if he was hunted by another man. It would be a frightening experience. It would be more frightening though if the man being pursued was unaware of his danger.

For a moment her mind went back to the conversation at the dinner table. Wasn't that *californio* bandit, Sabás Orozco, in exactly that predicament? Hadn't she, in effect, put John Leslie on *his* trail? For the sake of money?

And wasn't that worse, to track down a man to kill him just for financial gain, than what Sutter was doing it for — vengeance?

It made her feel unclean, inhuman. She could blame her awakened feeling partly on the attitude of her women boarders, or Miss

Hanna at least, who so obviously had held sympathy for Tiburcio Vásquez. Was she, Belle, less a woman for what she had done? Oh God, she thought, I wish I had never told Johnny about that reward.

Still, that would have had little bearing on Benteen's, Sutter's, quest for revenge. He would have sought out Johnny no matter where he was, no matter what he was doing.

He was only waiting for a clue as to where Johnny was, she thought. He suspected that she knew, and he was waiting for her to reveal it.

How could she warn Johnny without giving him away?

On the second day, Benteen questioned her. He sought her out after the other boarders had left.

"Interesting table talk last evening," he said. "I was some surprised at the schoolmarm's romantic notions about that Mex bandit."

"A foolish girl, Mr. Benteen. But there are others like her. Vásquez, despite his desperate career, proved to be a rather charming rogue as a prisoner. Even his jailers grew to like him. And there was no doubting his courage."

"Most men admire courage," he said. "But I didn't realize it was so important to women."

"It has its importance. However, there was

more than that about him. Charisma, I believe, is a word I have heard Miss Hanna use to describe him."

"Charisma?"

"Something hard to define, I think. But it was the source of his appeal for many."

"And this Orozco? Does he have it?"

"Possibly. For his own kind, the *californios,* at least. We will not know about the Americans probably, until he is taken."

"That brings me to a question," Benteen said. "That marshal from Jericho, Leslie — the one who is soft on you —"

"Mr. Benteen!"

"He was heading this way. Do you reckon he might have heard about the reward on this Orozco?"

"I told you he hadn't been here."

"So you did, so you did." He kept staring at her.

She couldn't stand his silence. She said, "Why would he care about it?"

"Bounty, Belle, bounty. Word in Jericho was that he wasn't only fed up with marshaling. Word was that he was hoping to do better out here. Moneywise, I mean. A little like my own intentions, I might say."

Her alarm grew. Even if he had no idea where Johnny was, if they both set out after the outlaw — She said, "I suppose there will be many taking up his trail now. Orozco's, I mean."

"Who else but Orozco's?" he said, staring again. When she made no reply, he went on, "But most of those taking after him won't know the desert like I do."

"You do not know the Mojave, Mr. Benteen."

"I know Arizona, ma'am. From one end to the other. I doubt the Mojave can be much different." He paused. "I have tracked down Apaches for the army. I can track a Mexican bandit, I'm sure."

"Why do you tell me this?"

"If your man, Leslie, should have it in mind to do the same, we could maybe team up and split the reward." He paused again. "Belle, I think you know more about him than you're telling."

She shook her head vigorously, affecting exasperation.

He still kept staring.

She made her decision then. He was wearing her down with his probing. Sooner or later she would let slip the information he was seeking, and then it would be too late to warn Johnny.

She would have to go to Sierra Gorda and alert Johnny of his danger. If she was lucky, she would have a day or two's lead.

CHAPTER 3

The day he left Belle's, John Leslie caught the Southern Pacific north through the two-year-old San Fernando tunnel and up the western fringe of the desert to the town of Mojave. Here the railroad turned westward to wind its way tortuously through the Tehachapis and into the San Joaquin Valley. Passengers heading north through the desert left the train at Mojave and went by stagecoach toward Owens Valley, east of the High Sierras range. This was also the route to Sierra Gorda.

It was the afternoon of the second day when the Concord stage climbed the Yellow Toll Road and reached the mining site.

At once Leslie felt almost at home. Sierra Gorda, Jericho, a half dozen other mining towns he had been in, they all ran to sameness, he thought.

The stage stopped in front of the American Hotel, a substantial board-sided building of two floors, a sign that the camp had visions of permanence.

And why not? He had heard talk on the route up that the bullion coming out of the seven hundred claims on the mountain had

reached in a previous year two million dollars.

Of these claims, he learned that three were
by far the most important. They were the
Santa Ynez, the San Juan, and the Anglo.

Leslie mused over the names and wondered
briefly if the names reflected the blood of
the discoverers. Two Mexican, one *yanqui,*
maybe. He knew the first discoveries were
made by earlier Mexican prospectors. The
third with the Yankee name made him wonder. Had it been bought by a gringo, or stolen
by him? One way or another it seemed, the
gringos eventually got it all. This was true
of the silver mines, as it had earlier been true
of the great Mexican grant ranchos.

He had scarcely got out of the Concord
when he was accosted by a short, muscular
man with a familiar face and a Cornish accent.
He searched his memory for the name of the
man, a miner by his clothes.

The miner had no hesitancy. "John Leslie,
sir! Remember me? From five years back in
the thriving town of Jericho, it was. My name
is —"

"Will Stoke," Leslie said.

"So. You have a good memory, Marshal,
seeing as you only had cause to learn my name
a time or two. And that while upholding the
law against the disturbing of the peace."

Leslie extended his hand.

"It's a fine thing to see you again, sir," Stoke said. "Be you coming here to control this town?"

"Control the town?"

"Aye. Bring some law, sir. By God, this place needs a bit of it. We had a sheriff's deputy till last month, but he was killed by a highwayman robbing the stage while he was a passenger. Since then we've not had a replacement sent us by the county sheriff at Independence."

"Why the delay?"

"They say the sheriff is looking for a man as can suit the job. There are some mean buggers here, preying on us honest miners. But then, I suppose you'd be knowing all about that, eh, sir?"

"No," John Leslie said. "I didn't come to hire out my gun."

"What then, sir? What else would you be doing in a mining town like Sierra Gorda?"

That was a question that had entered Leslie's own mind.

He was here to be in proximity to that Mexican bandit, Orozco's depredations, but in the meantime —

"The town could certainly use a man of your talents," Stoke said. "And I would gladly bring up your name to the camp council, on which sit several of the important operators here."

"I'll think about it, Will," Leslie said.

"Do that, sir. And it is a fine thing to be seeing you again."

Leslie nodded and walked into the hotel. He was thinking, for chrissake! What am I considering? He had quit Jericho because he felt his ability was fading — well, that was only part of the reason. The real reason was Belle. His wanting her had never left him, and now she was to be had.

But first he wanted to save the business she had worked so hard for. To do that he was intending to pit himself against a dangerous outlaw with a big price on his head. What was so different between that and wearing a marshal's star again? At least wearing it temporarily, until he learned something about the bandit's way of operation.

A man had to eat, and the cost of living in a boomtown like Sierra Gorda was bound to be high. The sheriff, Stoke had said, was going to send a replacement lawman when one was available. Leslie just might fill in while he waited for Orozco's next strike. He knew from experience that where there were miners, there were weekly payroll shipments coming in. Those shipments would be strong bait for a man like Orozco.

★ ★ ★

Sierra Gorda had transformed from camp to town. Its main street was lined with wood buildings. False-fronted stores, restaurants, and saloons had replaced the earlier canvas shacks scattered about the barren mountainside.

Two stages daily from Owens Valley, five thousand feet below, made the climb to serve it. And food and provisions arrived in an endless chain by the returning fourteen- and sixteen-mule freight wagons, the same wagons that hauled the bullion down to the railhead at Mojave. Bullion from the smelters below Sierra Gorda, owned by a man named Amos Barker. The ore from the mines reached those smelters by aerial tramway buckets, a system devised and also owned by Barker.

The bullion was cast into ingots eighteen inches long, weighing eighty-five pounds and, depending on their silver content, worth twenty to thirty-five dollars each.

The farmers of the Los Angeles area found an ever increasing market for their produce in the Sierra Gorda-bound wagons. Sacks of flour, sugar, potatoes, and nuts, barrels of wine, crates of fruit, and bales of hay — every staple item from picks to crated chickens tolled north toward the mountain.

As Belle had told Leslie, the silver of Sierra Gorda had made the old pueblo of Los Angeles grow.

It had also drawn the predators.

The town council met in an empty dining alcove of the American Hotel. Present were John Leslie and Will Stoke, who had been invited for the purpose of introducing Leslie and recounting his qualifications.

As they seated themselves around a large table, Leslie by habit chose a chair nearest the room corner, giving him a view of the double doorway into the main dining area.

It was something a man did instinctively when he had worn the star in a tough mining town.

A large man in a frock coat, trim-bearded, broad-shouldered, florid-faced, and well-fed nodded toward Stoke.

The Cornishman appeared somewhat abashed in the company he was in, but he spoke up strongly as he presented Leslie to the half dozen others. "You are in need of a man able to control the wild element here till we get back our county law," he said. "For that job I can highly recommend the former marshal of Jericho, Arizona Territory, John Leslie."

The large man, who seemed to be the one

used to taking charge, said, "Name of Barker, Amos Barker. I own the Anglo Mine. John Leslie, eh? Your reputation is not unknown to me, even before Stoke here apprised us of your qualifications. I have heard your name mentioned on occasion. One of that growing breed that seems to have started with men like Hickok. Town-tamers, I believe I have heard them called."

John Leslie did not feel an answer was expected. He gave a brief nod and remained silent.

Barker went on, "I will introduce the others here. Around the table: Corbett, DeJong, Ryerson, and Thomas. All mine or business owners."

"Five men."

"Including myself, yes."

"Five men for seven hundred working claims."

"Any more would be cumbersome," Barker said. "What are you driving at?"

Leslie let his eyes sweep around the circle of men. He said, "All whites, I see."

Barker frowned. "That bothers you?"

"I understand some of the smaller claims are owned and operated by Mexicans. Yet it appears they have no representation on this council. Half the men I've seen on the street are Mexican."

"And why should that concern you?"

"When you have a town split into two nationalities, and only one has any say about the running of it, it can cause a bitterness that can lead to serious trouble."

"Trouble," Barker said, "is what we are hiring you to control."

"With the Mexicans?"

"If it comes to that. So far it hasn't. They don't like us and we don't like them. Aside from a few small claim operators, they are mostly laborers in our employ. So far few have had the guts to make us trouble."

"I have known a lot of Mexicans," Leslie said. "You are a fool if you doubt their courage."

Barker looked angered by Leslie's choice of words. He said, "Forget the Mexicans. Your main job will be to keep the criminal element under control. They flock to a boomtown like flies to a privy. They prey on the men we've got working our mines. The usual riffraff of crooked gamblers, drunk rollers, cutthroats, and armed robbers. It plays hell with the town's morale — costs us money in lost efficiency of workers."

"I am familiar with these things."

Barker stared at him. "Stoke recommends you from an earlier acquaintance. I am bothered by one thing — why did you leave Arizona? Jerome, was it?"

"Jericho."

"Why?"

"A man wants a change now and then."

"Why come to Sierra Gorda? One mining town is pretty much like another."

Leslie said, "I don't know what Stoke told you, but I didn't come up here looking to hire on as marshal."

"Why then?"

"I came looking for Orozco."

They were all silent.

Barker was the only one who finally spoke. When he did, there was a hint of despisement in his tone. "You are after his bounty."

"Why not?"

"Stoke did not say you were also a bounty hunter."

"Stoke didn't know it."

Somebody at the table said, "How many men have you brought in for their pelts, Leslie?"

"Does it matter?"

Barker said, "No, I suppose not. Except where it interferes with your job of keeping the law here. Then we would have to fire you."

"When that time comes, and I hope it will be soon, I will resign," Leslie said. When nobody answered immediately, he said, "Take it or leave it, gentlemen."

Barker said, "I move we take it. The job is only temporary at best, until the Inyo County sheriff gets a man for us."

"I am in agreement with that," Leslie said.

For the first time Barker smiled faintly. "The reason we accept you on your own terms should be obvious to you. If you can rid us of that Mexican bastard Orozco, you'll be doing us more good than merely keeping the camp under control. You might be interested to know that I personally have added a thousand dollars to the governor's price on his head."

"He must have hit your payroll or ingot shipments pretty hard," Leslie said.

"He's never got to the payroll money, though he's come close several times. Always picked the wrong stages. He has carried off a couple of ingots now and then." Barker scowled. "No, it was something else. The son of a bitch Mex held up a stage I was on down near Coyote Holes and stole my favorite pocket watch. And refused to give it back." Barker paused. "You know what he said when I told him it was a prized heirloom from my grandfather? He said, 'So would have been the ranch of my own grandfather, which you sons of whores gringos stole from him.' "

Leslie was thoughtful. He said, "So if I

should bring him in alive, I'd get three thousand from the state and a thousand from you."

Barker shook his head. "No. If you bring him in *dead,* you'll only get two thousand from the state, but you'll get a thousand from me."

"You want him dead?"

"Of course I want him dead!" Barker said. "I told you, the thieving Mex stole my watch!"

Sierra Gorda had not become a boomtown overnight. The mining camp high on the mountain was slow to evolve.

It had been twelve years since a Mexican prospector named Luis Fuentes staked the first claim there and began slowly to develop it. He was poor, and only after much hard work, and the help of his family members, did he begin to extract a moderate amount of ore each day. He processed it there on the side of the mountain in crude, hand-built adobe and rock ovens called by the Mexicans *vasos.* His mine was a "coyote mine," so-called because its crooked trenches which followed the surface veins looked like the diggings of coyotes.

He called his mine the San Juan.

He packed his crude ingots down the mountain by mule to Fort Independence, from where they could be freighted southward to Los Angeles.

Amos Barker at that time was a successful merchant and sutler at the fort. What the Mexicans were doing caught his interest at once.

Within a few weeks he opened a store on the mountain, gambling the site had a future and determined to share it. His operating procedure was simple and worked well. He gave easy credit to Fuentes and other Mexicans then developing claims, until they had overdue accounts of more than two thousand dollars. Then he went to the county court at Independence and got judgments against them for what they owed. What he got in settlements were interests in three of the potentially richest mines at the workings, the San Juan, the Santa Ynez, and the Estrella.

In this he was only following the methods of earlier *yanquis* who had similarly wrested the old grant ranchos from the Mexican dons.

All the mines showed promising silver quartz veins along their burrowings. But the Estrella had something more — the largest lode of galena, or silver-lead ore, on the mountain.

Barker had studied silver, and he knew that galena held a key to riches. He knew how essential lead was in the smelting of silver ore, and that the man who built a smelter and controlled the galena deposits would eventually control most of Sierra Gorda's silver.

He promptly renamed the Estrella. He called it now, the Anglo.

He had several tons of Anglo ore processed in the *vasos,* freighted to Los Angeles, then sent by ship to San Francisco, where he had financial contacts.

The crude ingots became collateral samples for the capital he needed to finance a real smelter and to build a steep wagon road up from the floor of Owens Valley. The road he routed through a narrow canyon just below the camp, and he began collecting toll on everything that moved to or from the mines.

The smelter he built at the bottom of the grade. To bring the ore down to it, his own or, at a price, that of others, he built the steam-operated aerial tramway.

By the time of John Leslie's arrival, Amos Barker was king of the mountain at Sierra Gorda.

Still it was a wide-open town. The lawless element had found its remote desert location a reasonably safe refuge. Shootings were a regular thing. The slain deputy-in-residence had not attempted to apprehend outlaws; his orders were to maintain a loose semblance of law so the mines could function.

Whiskey and whores made the saloons and dance halls, and the brothels of such as Lulu

Trudeau and Maggie Morgan, the frequent scenes of gunfights.

All this John Leslie soon found out. Christ! he thought, I've made a bad decision. In the ten years after he had first tamed Jericho, he had been accustomed to only sporadic action. His reputation there had kept the rowdies in line except for rare occasions, such as the incident with the Bodie Kid.

Here he was confronted by a town bigger and wilder than Jericho at its worst. And though he had tamed Jericho, he had been ten years younger and faster when he did it.

Still he had his pride. Will Stoke had started to spread his reputation through the town, and now it was up to him to live up to it. He had wanted out when he'd left Jericho. But now he was back in — like a damn fool, he told himself — and his pride would not let him quit without making his try at doing the job they had hired him for.

It was a big strike, Sierra Gorda was, he thought. The biggest silver strike since the Comstock up in Nevada. The Comstock had made San Francisco grow. The Sierra Gorda was doing the same for Los Angeles, although it was, as yet anyway, only a fraction of the Comstock's size.

There was another thing he had not sensed so strongly in Arizona, the resentment of the

Mexicans toward the gringos.

There was a reason for this, of course. In Arizona the whites had come and taken from the Indians. There had been few, if any, rich Mexican or Spanish rancheros there to be swindled.

But California was different. Everyone knew of the Mexican land grantees, the aristocratic dons of old pastoral California. And how the sharp Yankee traders had come and taken it all away from them.

There was a smoldering fire of resentment that would not die out. It burst into flare in scattered ways. In a town like Sierra Gorda, where half the labor force was Mexican or Mexican *californio*, you got the feeling that the fire smoldered under a powder keg.

This was an element new to Leslie's experience. It was something he wondered how he would handle if the explosion came.

His first night as marshal he almost found out.

He was making his rounds and, coming to the front of the Sonora Palace, heard an altercation inside. He stepped in and was confronted by a Mexican girl, stiletto in hand, lashing out at a gringo miner, a huge man with the build of a bear.

Despite his bulk the man moved nimbly backward to escape her first thrust. But she was a slim and angry girl and she moved faster than he with her second attempt and slashed his arm. Blood spurted from it.

Leslie pulled his gun and yelled, "Drop it!"

The girl ignored him. She leaped forward in another attack as the big miner, now scared, stumbled back.

She would have knifed him then, had not a full-figured blonde in tight dance hall dress grabbed her from behind and twisted her wrist and wrested the weapon from her. "You crazy Mex bitch," the big blonde said.

A Mexican suddenly had a gun in his hand. He pointed it at the miner and said, "You gringo bastard! You insult my girl!" He fired a shot and missed.

Leslie moved fast then. Afraid to fire in the crowded dance hall, mixed with both *yanqui* and Mexican miners and their dance partners, he stepped forward and brought his gun barrel down hard on the Mexican's arm. The Mexican's gun flew from his hand, struck the floor, and fired a round on impact.

The bullet struck the Mexican girl in the buttocks, and she let out a scream that froze everybody in the place.

And then there was a rush of Mexicans for Leslie, as one of them called something out in Spanish.

Leslie caught enough to know he'd yelled

the marshal had shot the girl. Leslie cursed under his breath and fired a shot over the heads of the group surging toward him.

That stopped them.

There were accusations and denials flung back and forth then. And gradually Leslie brought them down to a measure of calm.

A self-proclaimed doctor, a gringo, among the dancers offered to attend the Mexican girl's wound. And Leslie did not stop to argue about the offer. He put his gun on the big miner and ordered him out, and together they withdrew.

Outside he said to the big man, "You goddamn fool! Starting trouble in a Mex dance hall!"

"All I did was pinch her butt," the big miner said.

"That's all it takes sometimes," Leslie said. "Stay out of there from now on."

"Hell, you don't have to tell me that," the miner said. He went ambling up the street, looking more than ever like a bear.

"The goddamn fool!" Leslie said again, trying to relieve his nerves. He knew that from now on the Mexicans of Sierra Gorda would be against him.

He was not like Belle. He did not have her tolerance for the *californios,* because he knew

56

only by hearsay of the purported injustices done them. In Jericho there had been no overt racial conflict. The Mexicans there had kept to themselves and, though he had sometimes gone into the *barrio* to arrest one for disturbing the peace, they had made him no real trouble. He had suspected a certain amount of resentment existed, but it had been kept hidden.

The Mexicans of Jericho had been mostly migrants from below the border, and they did not have the reasons to hate the *yanquis* that the native *californios* had.

Now he walked constantly on the alert.

And he cursed himself for a fool for pinning on the star again. Still he knew it was something he was driven to do, just as he was driven to go after the bandit Orozco.

He had quit once and, so doing, he had lost the self-esteem by which he had lived. Now, although he had angered the *californios* perhaps, he had handled his first incident well he thought. He had a new feeling of some pride regained.

And then the rumors started coming to him.

Will Stoke was the first to bring them. "John Leslie, sir," Stoke said, "it is to be warning you of a new danger that I be coming to you now. The affair at the Palace the other evening has brought it on."

"I thought it was settled well enough," Leslie said.

"And so it was, sir, to an extent. But the Mexicans have among them a champion of sorts, one they call a *machón*. His name is Luis Rios, a real bully boy among his kind. An extortionist of sorts, I'd say, who lives off his pickings on the *cantina* owners. He never bothers the whites, and so he has been left alone."

"So where do I come in?" Leslie said.

"The word is around that he's bragging he'll take care of you, Marshal. It would make him an even bigger threat among his kind, as you may well understand."

"Take care of me how?"

"He is said to be a *pistolero* of some repute, sir. Even as yourself. He's rumored to have killed twenty men in Sonora or some other outlandish place."

Another Bodie Kid? Leslie thought. Only this time more than an incompetent kid. This time a qualified reputation seeker. A *pistolero* who could put him to the test.

"He is not a *californio* then?"

"A Sonoran, I believe."

"I've known Sonorans in Arizona," Leslie said.

"As have I," Stoke said. "But, Marshal, none like this. He is cut from a different cowhide, this one." Stoke paused. "He makes the Sonora Palace his hangout, John, and it's lucky you were, I think, that he wasn't there the other evening during the fuss." He hesitated again. "Not that you wouldn't have been his match, I'm thinking, but because he would likely have shot you in the back."

And now Leslie carried his threat with him as he made his rounds.

He kept remembering that day when Bert Sutter had thrown down on him with his new Peacemaker in Jericho. Would he better cope this time if or when he was put to the test? He determined not to be surprised. But would his reflexes betray him as they had that other time? That was his real fear.

He did not have to wait long to find out.

It was just past noon, and Leslie was making his first round of the day. Because he could not afford not to be seen there, he made the Palace in the Mexican section his first destination.

And Luis Rios was waiting for him out front.

A group of *californios* were lounging with him as Leslie started down the street. He could see them waiting, but he did not know Rios by sight, and he did not know of his presence there until the others split away, leaving the machón standing alone.

Rios was a big man but not fat. He wore *charro* garb that flaunted his culture among the drab gringo clothing of the others, mine laborers by their looks.

He was a man of guts, Leslie knew at once, as Rios stepped off the portico and into the street.

"*Hola!* Marshal," Rios said. "You come to see me?"

"No," Leslie said. "I'm just making my rounds."

"Too bad. Because I been want to see you."

"I'm here, then."

"I don't like what you do the other night," Rios said. "You get rough with Mexicans here in the Palace. Is bad."

Leslie knew it had to come. He said, "Well?"

Luis Rios grabbed for his pistol, worn high on his hip.

Leslie this time was ready. He put a shot into Rios's breastbone that knocked him back and down.

Rios did not move again.

Leslie turned to face the Mexicans watching from the portico. They were staring at him. From that distance he could not be sure what he was seeing in their faces.

He thought, though, that it was respect.

CHAPTER 4

The Concord in which Belle was riding halted, and the driver swore.

Six Indians surrounded the stage. They all looked drunk, some swaying in their saddles. The saddles were fairly good and so were their horses. Not their own, the stage driver thought. The bastards probably stole them from one of our stations. Likely they're down from Mono Lake. Mono Paiutes. Not too dangerous when they're sober. Drunk, that was a different matter.

"Don't make no sudden moves," the driver called to his passengers. "Let me do the talking."

The passengers got out. There was a whiskey drummer in a checkered suit. A cattle rancher in a broad-brimmed Stetson and fancy boots — down from Bridgeport, likely, the driver thought. A mine superintendent. And the handsome woman who'd told him she was up from L.A. and headed for Sierra Gorda, for what reason he did not know.

She was the one that seemed to catch the eyes of the Paiutes, and the driver swore again.

The whiskey drummer smelled like he'd been sampling his own wares, and now he couldn't keep his mouth shut. He said, "Injuns, ain't they?"

The driver said, "Shut up!"

"Paiutes?"

"I reckon."

"Well then," the drummer said, and turned toward them. "Chief Winnemucca, him great chief," he said to one who appeared to be the leader.

The lead Paiute raised a rifle and shot him through the chest. The drummer fell backward into the roadway and lay gurgling his life away.

Goddamnit! the driver thought. A lot of Paiutes got no use for the Nevada chief. They figure he sold them out.

The mine superintendent and the cattle rancher had more sense. They looked tense, but they kept their mouths shut.

The woman didn't. "You bastards!" she yelled, half mad and half about to cry.

The Paiutes all began to laugh. One of them, not the leader, suddenly spurred toward her. He leaped down, grabbed her in his arms, and tossed her over his saddle. He was very strong, as if he might have spent some time bucking bales of hay on some white man's ranch. He swung up behind her and, as she struggled to slide off, he smashed his fist behind her ear and knocked her out. The other Paiutes laughed some more.

The cattleman reached for the gun at his hip. The Paiute who had killed the drummer killed him too.

The mine superintendent, who had looked like a courageous man about to act, now looked pale and scared.

The driver felt he had to say something. He said to the lead Paiute, "You've had your fun. Give back the woman and let us go."

"Sure," the Indian said. "We have fun. But we have more fun with woman. But you go now. We catch you again sometime. Maybe you bring more white woman, hey?"

The mine superintendent started to get into the stage.

"Hey! You, no," the lead Paiute said.

The mining man's nerve was gone. He said weakly, "I got money. Take it. We make a trade." He reached inside his suit coat and the Paiute shot him too. The mine superintendent's hand came out of his coat as he fell and he dropped the wallet he had been grasping for.

"Oh hell," the Paiute said to nobody. "I thought he got a gun there."

The other Paiutes laughed uproariously, as if it was a big joke. The leader didn't. He got down and rolled the dead mine superintendent over and took the wallet and shoved it into the pocket of the dirty Levi's he was wearing. He looked up and saw the stage driver staring at him and looking sick, and he said, "Hey! You go now. Next time bring more white woman."

The driver climbed back up on his seat and started up the team. He didn't look back. There wasn't any reason to, he told himself. The three men passengers were dead. And the woman — He cursed himself for a coward. But what could he do?

From behind a screening of greasewood on the bench above a dry wash cut through colored sandstone cliffs, a horseman wearing a sombrero had watched it all. It was no coincidence that he was there.

He had been waiting himself in Red Rock Canyon for the stage to arrive. He had been waiting for it for several hours when the cursed Paiutes had suddenly ridden down from the north and spoiled his plans. Trust the stupid *indios* to ruin everything, he thought.

He thought about the woman they had taken. He did not move for some time. Then, as if reaching a decision, he touched spurs to his black gelding and began to follow the Paiutes' tracks.

They did not lead far. Less than a half mile away the Paiutes halted in a narrow canyon where the angle of the sun caused one wall to give some shade to the bottom. Trust a Paiute to find shade where there was none, the rider on the black horse thought. Well, why not? The desert was their habitat. Even as it had become his own.

In some ways he was already smarter than the Paiutes when it came to surviving in the great wasteland. He knew enough to always scan his back trail. Of course the Paiutes were drunk, and that made a difference.

He knew they were drunk because of the way they were yelling now as they spread the woman out on the sand of the canyon floor, two holding her struggling body while a third got himself ready to mount her.

For a moment the rider on the black horse could not move, stricken immobile by his own desire as he watched. Then cursing, he raised the new Winchester carbine he had recently stolen and, levering fast after each shot, he executed each Paiute in turn.

Belle watched as he made the small fire of brush and set the frying pan to balance on the three rocks he had pulled together to form a crude stove. So far he had said almost nothing through the long afternoon ride after he had shot the Paiutes. He had simply helped her on one of their horses, selected two more for spares, tied the lead rope of one to her saddle, and led off into the desert.

At first she had thought possibly he did not know her language. But finally, after she had got over the great shock of her ordeal, she had tried to thank him, despite the fear he had evoked in her by the casual way he had dispatched the Paiutes.

He had spoken then in accented English. "You come with me, gringa lady. I am Sabás. Sabás Orozco. Your name?"

"Belle," she said. Orozco! She trembled as with a chill.

"Bell? Like *campana* in the church?" His tone was polite.

"No. Not like that. *Belle*." She owed her life to him, she thought.

"Me, I don't understand."

"*Belle*." She tried to think of the Spanish words she'd learned in Los Angeles. She said after a pause, "I think like *bella*, maybe."

"Ah, *bella!* Means beautiful. Good name for you." He showed white teeth beneath a trim black mustache. His dark eyes seemed to show amusement. "*Bella!*"

"*Belle*," she said, wondering why she corrected him.

"So. *Belle*."

"Where are you taking me?"

He did not answer at once. Then he said, "You like to be raped by Paiutes, Belle?"

"Of course not!"

"Maybe you like me better than them, eh?"

The chill came back as she pondered his meaning. She decided to ignore his implication. "Of course. You saved me from them."

He grinned. "So. You owe me, eh?"

Her fear made her angry. "I gave you my thanks."

"*Sí*. But later maybe you thank me better?" He laughed and spurred his horse a little ahead of hers.

There was nothing she could do but follow.

Now, as he made camp, she was wondering if this was the time he meant by later. *Sabás Orozco!* The name alone frightened men. Still, she thought, his appearance was not what she would have expected. He was younger, for one thing. No older than she. And handsome. She thought maybe this was why the remnants of the old *californio* families aided him, offered him refuge when he was hard-pressed.

Another thought struck her, and she said, "Is it true, Mr. Orozco, that you are descended from the *californios?*"

He smiled. "You goddamn gringos. Always respect for the dons. After you robbed them of their holdings. But never respect for a poor

Mexican." He paused. "Yes, I am born of *californios*. But not like you think. My father and my grandfather, they were poor Mexicans like me. One difference. They had work. As vaqueros. Vaqueros for the dons. A vaquero, *bella* gringa lady, he was always poor, but he got his pride. You understand? He is a man. Now, no more chance for a Mexican vaquero. What's a poor Mexican going to do, eh?"

Belle said, "There is work in the farmers' fields in the San Joaquin, even around Los Angeles there is work. And there is work in the mines."

He turned and stared at her for a long time without speaking. Then he said, "So, maybe you can say I work the mines, eh? But not with pick and shovel." He slipped his revolver from its holster. "I work the mines sometimes with this. The pay is not always good. But it makes the goddamn gringos mad."

She was afraid again. She said, "If you hate gringos, you don't want to keep me. Let me go."

"Well, I hate gringos. But I don't hate *gringas*. And an hombre like me, roaming out here in the desert, he can't be choosy, eh?"

Despite her fear, his words piqued her. She bit her lip. If she spoke then, she might say something that would enrage him.

He said, "You are good cook?"

She gave him a short nod.

"Good. Is bacon in my saddlebags. Beans. Flour. Coffee. Water in canteens. From now on is your job, Belle."

"I never cooked over a campfire."

"You learn, Belle. You don't learn, you don't eat."

He watched her hands as she prepared the meal. On the ring finger of her right hand he saw the plain gold band. "You married woman? You wear ring on wrong hand."

"I'm a widow."

"Widow? Ah, *viuda*. How long since you don't got a husband?"

"Three years."

"Ah! You been a long time with no hombre, eh? Me, I been a while with no woman." He paused. "You like the desert, Belle?"

"No."

"Well, you get used to."

"What do you mean?"

"What I say. You get used to."

"To the desert?"

"Sure. To the desert. And to me too. You my woman now, Belle."

"I am not!"

He grinned. "Well, maybe I find more Paiutes. Give you back. You want that?"

It was the stage driver who brought the

news of the Paiute attack and the abduction of Belle to the camp at Sierra Gorda.

"Paiutes?" somebody said. "Hell, there ain't been no trouble with them for a long time."

The driver turned and looked at the speaker. "There won't be any trouble with this bunch again. Ever."

"What do you mean?"

"I hadn't left and gone a half mile before all hell busted loose with rifle fire." He hesitated. "I went back — on account of the woman. I couldn't just leave without knowing —"

"What the hell happened?"

"Mexican riding a big black horse killed the bunch of them Injuns and rode off with her his own self. Orozco."

"Orozco? You sure?"

"Hell yes, I'm sure. I been robbed twice by that bastard. I ain't about to forget what he looks like. But what the hell could I do, me against him, and me without even a riding horse? About the woman, I mean." He scanned the group around him. "She was on her way here when them Paiutes struck. Name of Belle Jackson, if I remember."

"Belle?" John Leslie stepped forward. "Where did it happen?"

"Red Rock Canyon. Orozco and the woman, they rode off east into the desert."

70

"Rode off together?"

"Hell, he done just rescued her from them raping savages. No telling how she must have felt, right about then. Besides, she wasn't in no position to protest, I reckon. What would you have done?"

"Don't know," a miner said. "I ain't ever been raped by a Paiute." He chuckled.

Leslie said tightly, "There's nothing funny here."

The miner looked at him, at the star he was wearing, at his low-slung gun. "You're right, Marshal, there sure as hell ain't. I don't rightly know why I said that. You want to get up a posse, I'll be the first to ride with you."

The stage driver said, "No posse yet ever caught up with Orozco. Ain't hardly nobody ever seen him even, except for stage men like me and passengers and freighters and station keepers and such."

"I've been your marshal here for only a couple of weeks," Leslie said. "But I'm resigning as of now. Belle is the woman I figure to marry."

"You going to take to Orozco's trail alone?"

"You just said no bunch ever caught up with him."

"That's a fact, Marshal."

"Well then, you see what I've got to do."

The stage driver said, "I got no love for

71

Orozco. But it appears he done your woman a favor, comes to them Paiutes."

"What I'm wondering about," another miner said, "is what Orozco's intentions with her are?"

Leslie's jaw tightened. He had a damn good idea.

Barker came up. "What's the fuss here, Marshal?"

Leslie gestured toward the stage driver.

Barker looked at the driver. "Well?"

The driver repeated his story. Barker cursed.

Leslie said, "I'm going after him, Mr. Barker. He's got the woman I came to California to marry."

Barker stared thoughtfully at him. "Yeah. Well, we ought to have that deputy up here from Independence soon. You think you can get that Mexican bastard?"

"I've got to get him," Leslie said. "He's got my woman."

"Nobody's yet been able to get him."

"He's got my woman," Leslie said again.

"Yeah. I guess that could make the difference. Keep you on his trail, no matter how tough the desert is. It's the desert that beats most who go after him."

The man who called himself Benteen looked

up from the table toward the new woman who was serving the meal to him and the other boarders. He said, "Where's Belle?"

The girl was in her twenties, slightly resembled Belle but without her fine looks. She said, "I'm Ruthie. Belle's cousin. I'll be filling in for a few days. Belle had to make a trip."

"A trip? Where?"

"Up to the mines. To Sierra Gorda."

"Why?"

The girl suddenly seemed to realize she had said too much. "I don't know why."

Benteen gave her his best smile. "Sorry. No offense, Ruthie. I was just curious, is all."

He'd talk to the girl later. He knew her kind. Starved for compliments probably, plain as she was. He'd always had a way with women, he told himself. But he'd had mighty few chances to use it.

An army post was a damn poor place to meet them. There was laundry row with its washerwomen who were often noncoms' wives, and you could get killed that way.

And there were officers' wives, and you couldn't get within touch range of any of them, no matter how bad you wanted to — or, sometimes, how bad some of them wanted you to, he thought. There were too many eyes watching.

Sierra Gorda. Now why would Belle suddenly take off for there? He had known she was lying about John Leslie's whereabouts. He had tried to frighten her just enough to make her show her hand. Now she had.

He'd follow her to Sierra Gorda.

CHAPTER 5

John Leslie took the stage down from Sierra Gorda to the station nearest the scene of the Paiute attack. It was called Cantil. There he bought a saddle horse and a pack mule, a week's supply of grub, and three large canteens to fill with water.

The station keeper watched him curiously. "You ever been into the Mojave before?" he said.

Leslie shook his head. "I know something of the desert country over in the Territory, though."

"Might help," the station keeper said. "But you'll find this desert some different. For one thing, you'll not find any catch basins with water. No *tinajas*, you understand? None nowhere. Any sinkholes you find will be pure alkali."

"No *tinajas?*"

"Not on the Mojave. Not this time of year. The Paiutes call it the 'land of little rain.' Makes the Territory deserts look like an oasis."

"I'll try to remember that."

"Won't take no trying. A couple of days

out in it and you won't remember nothing else."

"Where's the spot the stage was held up?"

"Which time?"

"This last time. By the Paiutes."

"You passed it a few miles north up in Red Rock. If you can read trail sign, you'd ought to pick it out. We left them dead Paiutes lay. The buzzards may still be hanging around, help you find them." The station man paused. "You going after Orozco?"

"That was my woman he took."

"Damn Mexican," the station keeper said. "Still he done her a favor, killing them Paiutes."

"Many of them around?"

"First I heard of in years. At one time they used to come down from Mono and Nevada to Black Mountain in the El Pasos there beyond Red Rock. Figured it was some kind of holy peak. Made a pilgrimage to it, them that had religion. Don't come no more to my knowledge. Them bucks that took your woman was just a handful of drunk renegades looking for trouble."

"Looks like they found it. This Orozco, how does he live out there?"

"Keeps moving, I guess. Knows what few springs there is. Hits our stations, stages, even freighters. To tell the truth, I don't know *how* he lives out there. There's always a few prospectors roaming around and willing to trade a meal for loot he's taken, I reckon. But the real reason he can do it is he's part coyote."

"My woman," Leslie said, "he's got to feed her too." His deep worry was showing.

The station keeper saw it. "You better find him fast," he said. "Before he gets tired of her."

There was still enough sign around the attack scene so that Leslie could read it. He also followed the tracks into the canyon where the Paiutes had taken Belle and got themselves killed by Orozco.

There wasn't much meat left on the skeletons. The buzzards and the coyotes had taken care of that.

He picked up the trail there and followed it easterly along the south fringe of the El Pasos. The country was a desolate reach of sand and sage and greasewood, and only rarely an area where the twisted arms of Joshua trees shook their thorny fists at the fierce heat of a brassy sky.

Off to the south he could see the bare expense of a dry lake playa.

The thought of Belle out there in Orozco's hands was a constant goad to him. Even worse was the thought that he might abandon her. The station keeper's words "Before he gets tired of her" came back to him.

He swore at the outlaw until the thought came to him again that it was Orozco who had saved her from rape and likely death. He owed him thanks for that, and it mixed up his feelings so that he began to swear again.

He remembered the mature beauty of her, and he thought, he won't tire of her. For a moment he was relieved. Then he thought, Goddamnit! *No, he won't tire of her,* and raging jealousy destroyed his relief.

The trail was several days old now. He was lucky that there had been no violent windstorm to erase it. But in that length of time Orozco could have gone a long way. Unless he had dallied with Belle.

Benteen was two days behind Leslie. He talked to the same station keeper at Cantil. But the agent was not as free with his words as he had been with Leslie. There was something about this man that turned him close-mouthed.

Benteen had reached Sierra Gorda and learned of Belle's fate and of Leslie's taking up Orozco's trail. He had wasted no time, catching a return stage back to the station near the abduction site.

"I'll need a good horse, a pack animal, and provisions," he told the stationmaster. "I'm going into the desert to get that bandit."

"Don't have none left to sell you. Your best bet is the railhead at Mojave town."

"That's twenty miles south."

"This is a stage station. I keep relay teams, not much riding stock."

"At Sierra Gorda they told me the marshal had headed here to go after his woman."

"Yeah."

"You sold him a mount?"

"Only one I had. That and a pack burro a failed prospector sold me a while back."

"When did he leave?"

"Couple days back. You a friend of his?"

"Sure. That's why I want to help him find his woman."

"Well even so, you better stick with the stage to Mojave. Get what you need there."

"I'll lose another day at least."

"You don't have no choice. You better fit yourself out proper. The desert ain't no place for a greenhorn. Not this time of year especially."

Benteen's amber eyes bored into him. "Do I look like a greenhorn?"

The station keeper looked uneasy. "No, I reckon not." He hesitated, then said, "But if you go into the desert to help him, you must be a hell of a good friend."

"Bosom buddies," Benteen said. "I owe him something I'll never forget."

Leslie lost the trail on his second day. It led him into a labyrinth of rocky canyons where the tracks of Orozco and Belle disappeared. Leslie could see no reason for Orozco entering this maze unless it was to hinder possible pursuit.

He spent a couple of hours in futile search to find the lost trail and nearly lost himself before he decided to go back to the flat country, where a man could at least see.

Once there he rode again along the contour of the low range, his eyes always looking to pick out a sign that Orozco had come out again. He discovered nothing.

Christ! he thought, what a man needed for this was expert ability to read trail sign. That was something a town marshal did not acquire. He began now to doubt if he had the know-how to cope with the unknown Mojave. The thought that he might fail ate at his guts. A sense of inadequacy when Belle needed him most brought him to the edge of panic. I've got to find them, he thought. I've got to get her back. He kept on, following nothing.

Benteen had no such trouble. The sign to

him was as clear as if drawn on a map. He came to where Orozco had entered the terrain, saw that Leslie had followed. Benteen did not lose the trail, but he saw that Leslie had. He smiled grimly. To find his quarry was going to be easier than he had thought.

He ignored Orozco's trail and followed Leslie's as it led back out onto the desert floor. The damn fool is in over his head here, he thought. Benteen's concern now was that the desert might kill the bastard who had murdered his kid brother before he could do it.

Barely a kid, he thought bitterly, and drunk at that. Playacting a role inspired by rotgut liquor. And that goddamn small-time legend with a gun, John Leslie, had to shoot him in the guts. If he was as good as his legend, he could have handled the kid with a simple wound.

Did he know the pain of being gutshot? Benteen's face grew hard. His lips drew back until he bared his teeth. Benteen would see that he learned that pain. And soon.

Presently he saw the hoofprints of the horses, ridden and led by Orozco and the woman, come out of the rock country to rejoin those of his own quarry.

The reason was clear. They were heading toward a long, sloping pass which led northward through the range they had been skirting.

Benteen's excitement grew. He knew he had been gaining distance on Leslie. He began to hope he'd catch him on the other side of the pass.

"I'll get him, little brother," he said aloud. "I'll kill the murdering, star-packing bastard that shot you down."

He came out on the north slope of the pass summit. Below him dust had begun to swirl up from a faintly seen floor of a vast basin. Miles away and high above the thickening dust he could just make out the dark peaks of what must be the southern Sierra Nevadas.

Within moments they vanished from his sight, and he felt the first hard sting of gale-driven sand begin to strike his face, to fill his eyes.

He knew what that meant. A desert sandstorm was kicking up.

Leslie knew it too. But at first he ignored it, weighing the possibility that it would not be severe. His mind was on other things. His mind was on Belle. And on Orozco. And on what might be going on between them.

It went from there back to how it had been with Belle and himself in those earlier years. At thirty he had been a mature man. At twenty she had still been part girl, the naïve only child of a widowed cattle rancher. Her mother had died, when Belle was fifteen, from a fall off a horse. Her father had pretty much given up the struggle to make a go of his hardscrabble spread after that.

Then there had been an Apache raid while she was visiting friends in Jericho, a raid that left the ranch house burned down, her father dead inside it, the remaining livestock driven off.

At eighteen she was working as a waitress and cook in a Jericho restaurant.

Two years later John Leslie had drifted in and landed the job as marshal, because nobody else wanted it.

There had been real love between them, but she was too scarred by having lost those close to her by violent death. She would not risk it happening again.

Still, in time he would have convinced her to marry him, he was sure, had not Fred Jackson made his lucky strike and offered her a way out of the bleak country with its traumatic memories.

Her leaving had cut him deeply. She had been the one woman he had loved. Once she was gone, he had never really tried to find another. He had got his meager satisfaction, as most men did in the mining towns, from the women of the bordellos.

And now, when he had regained her, when what could have been was once more possible, he had lost her again. Lost her to an outlaw. There was an irony there, he thought. But it did not amuse him.

That last time, when it had been final, still choked him up as he thought about it. When she had said, "I can't live every day afraid I'll be a widow."

And he had said, "I can't give up what I am."

And she had said, "Then I'm sorry, John Leslie."

It had been an abrupt ending for what had been between them, an ending that never should have been. It had surprised him when she said that, and that made the hurt even worse.

He had felt that she would accept him as he was. That she was even proud of his standing in the town, that she shared somehow his pride in his profession, in the respect that was shown his ability with a gun.

None of it had come easy to him. He had never risen above the rank of private in the war. He had been in battles, but he had never suffered a wound. After the war he had drifted west, worked here and there on cattle spreads, become a just-fair cowhand with no particular talent for the job. He had tried his hand at mine work, but disliked to be underground, and gave it up.

When he hired on as lawman in Jericho, he had been no better than average with a handgun, and that wasn't very good. He had just happened to come by at the right time and was hired because he was medium tall, sinewy strong, with tanned, tough-looking features that impressed the members of Jericho's ad hoc council. That and because the marshal before him had been shot in the back while drinking in one of the saloons, and his murderer was hiding out in the local hills. A first condition of his hiring was that he go out and bring the killer in for trial.

He went out, but it didn't happen that way. The killer had put up a fight and Leslie, by a lucky shot, killed him and brought him in dead, and his reputation had begun.

He knew then what he had to do. He spent some of his time off for much of the first year, out away from the town, practicing until he became adept with the Starr Army .44 he'd carried since his war years. He had finally found his niche. One that gave him the prestige he had long craved.

And that was why he could not accede to Belle's condition that he give up wearing the star.

Besides, even up to the last when she told him she was going to marry Fred Jackson he'd continued to believe that she'd marry him. There was so much between them that he couldn't conceive of her putting it aside out of fear she'd become a widow. Hell, any man could die anytime. You could drop dead for no reason if you were selling ribbons in a dry goods store. As he had told her.

"It isn't the same thing at all!" Belle had said, and she had believed that.

Now following the lead of the bandit, Orozco, and fearful of what lay in her immediate future, her thoughts went to John Leslie, and to the day she had uttered those words. To the day her stubbornness had caused her to make the big mistake of her life. Because it was John Leslie she had wanted, not Fred Jackson.

She had not really realized her mistake until she and Fred reached Los Angeles and invested the money he'd received for his mining claim. Until they'd made the down payment on the boardinghouse and settled down to the humdrum existence of running it. The boredom was quickly too much for Fred, and it was a relief for both of them when he got the job freighting across the desert for Remi Nadeau.

Fred had been a surprise to her. Despite his likable personality and his measure of good looks, he was not of a passionate nature.

She had been a surprise to herself, too. Once married, she had discovered, and was even ashamed at, the strength of her own awakened desires. Fred's no way matched hers — he was an indifferent lover.

If he suspected she had made love with John Leslie before he arrived on the scene, Fred never voiced his suspicions. That was another display of his indifference. It further angered her, even as she was relieved that he made no issue of it. She really did not know why this was so. She only knew it was.

The long periods when he was gone on the twenty-odd-day trips to the mines and back were less stressful to her than those times when he had lain beside her night after night and only rarely made advances.

Those times had been humiliating to her, when overcome by her own desire, she in desperation had taken the initiative. They were even worse when she sometimes met with no reception.

There were other times, when he was gone on the desert and she had eligible male boarders, that she was tempted by her passion.

But she had refused to let herself become a wanton. And even after Fred died, she had held firmly to her code. Until the day that John Leslie had reentered her life.

That afternoon she had spent in his arms had set her aflame again. And then he, too, had left for the desert.

Yes, she had made love with Johnny before, discreetly, in Jericho. Before the realities of the prospect of marriage and her fear of the life he led as lawman began to interfere with their relationship.

Before Fred Jackson and his offer presented an easy escape from a hard decision.

Before she had become a fool.

Benteen, his eyes slitted against the stinging sand, was thinking back to how and why he had come to be where he was. The answer, of course, was Bert. Bert, and what Benteen had heard about his killing from that saloon owner in Jericho.

The saloon owner was a gambler named Slick Sam Fletcher, and he had been a friend of Bert's and one of the last men to speak with him before Bert had left the Fatima and gone out on the street that fateful noon to die.

Benteen did not know that Slick Sam Fletcher had also feuded occasionally with John Leslie over certain infractions of the rules laid down by the marshal. Such as the one that there be no crooked games. And that no liquor be served to falling-down drunks.

Benteen had stopped in the Fatima in mid-morning, and Fletcher was just opening up and taking an early stint at the bar until a hireling took over at noon. Benteen was his first customer at that hour.

Benteen ordered a drink, then said, "You know a kid named Bert Sutter?"

Sam Fletcher gave him a curious glance. "Used to," he said.

"He was working in these parts I heard."

"He was."

"He's gone?"

"You could say that." Fletcher was sizing him up. That went with his profession. He noted the campaign hat, had noticed the cavalry boots, appraised the general look of the man, and thought he had him pegged. "Working for the army?"

"Was." Benteen hesitated, then said, "Name of Sutter, Tom Sutter."

Quick interest showed in Slick Sam's eyes. "Related to Bert?"

"Brother."

Fletcher poured him another drink. "He was a hell of a good kid," he said.

Sutter stared at the saloon man's face. "*Was?*"

"I'm sorry, Sutter," Slick Sam said. "Bert

got himself killed a couple of months back."

"Bert? Killed?" Sutter's voice rose.

For a moment Fletcher thought he was going to be grabbed by the big man and hauled across the bar. He was ready to grab for the gun in the holster under his arm.

But Sutter did not make the move. Instead he said, "Tell me about it."

"You sure you want to hear?"

"I said I was his brother."

"That's why I asked." Fletcher nudged the bottle toward him, but Sutter's glass was still full.

"Well?" Sutter said.

"Happened about this time of day, maybe a little later. Bert had a drink or two here and walked out on the street, and got shot down."

"By who? They get the son-of-a-bitch? You got law here, ain't you?"

"Shot down in cold blood by the marshal himself," Slick Sam Fletcher said.

"What the hell for?"

"Trigger-happy."

"Bert? Bert was no hand with a gun!"

"I meant the marshal," Slick Sam said. "Proud of his rep, like a lot of small-town law-dogs are getting to be. Every time they make a kill, it makes their job a little easier. You can see how that'd be, can't you?"

90

Sutter's words came tightly. "What excuse did he give?"

"Claimed the kid drew first. I never believed that. Not Bert. Nicest kid I ever knew. First time I ever saw him wear a gun. Just bought it before it happened. Hell, he hadn't had time to learn to use it yet."

"You see it happen?"

"No, I was inside here along with most everybody else. We *heard* it happen and rushed out on the street, and there was Bert laying in the dust, moaning and crying and his guts running out of him through a hole in his belly. Made me sick."

Sutter looked pale and sick himself.

"Wasn't any witnesses on the street," the saloon man said. "Damn marshal gave his story, and you could believe it or not. Me, I never did."

Sutter's face had gone from pale to red. He grabbed up the glass from the bar and downed its contents. "Where can I find the son-of-a-bitch?" he said.

Slick Sam Fletcher told him.

CHAPTER 6

Orozco had brought her to the shelter of a cave where he had some stocked provisions. She had no idea where they were. He brought in enough greasewood branches for a fire to heat some canned food. He threw a saddle blanket on the stony ground for them to sit on while they ate. Despite her wariness of him Belle was starved from the long ride after her attack by the Paiutes.

"Good that you eat, Belle," he said. "You strong woman."

She said nothing and kept her eyes averted from his, avoiding his look.

He did not speak again until their meal was finished. Then he got a rolled blanket from where he had stacked the saddles and gear. The horses he had hobbled outside so they could forage the sparse bunchgrass.

He spread the blanket and looked at her again. This time, in sudden alarm, she stared at him and met his eyes.

"You tired, Belle?"

She was afraid to answer, but finally she said, "Of course. I'm not used to this life."

"You get used to," he said. "Like me."

"What are you going to do with me?"

He smiled. "Is lonely out here, Belle. Pretty soon you get lonely like me, maybe." He paused. "Why you been on that stage?"

She didn't know how to answer that. How could she tell him it was to warn a man who was out to kill him for the price on his head? She said, "I had business in Sierra Gorda."

"Business? What kind of business you have?"

"I was on my way to visit a friend."

"Hombre or woman?"

"A man."

"Ah! You in that kind of business, Belle?"

"No! That's not what I meant."

"*Sí.* I believe. You no *puta,* I can tell. But you long time without man."

That was true, she thought. Except for that one afternoon with Johnny, she had been without a man for three years. Her thoughts suddenly frightened her, more even than Orozco did.

"I be good to you, Belle."

"How is it that you speak good English?"

"Hell, I live around many gringos before. I work for some. They treat me like *mierda,* like they do most Mexicans."

"Are you any better off now?" she said.

He shrugged. "Maybe no. Pretty soon

93

maybe they catch me, and they hang me like they do Vásquez."

"Then why did you become a bandit?"

"I just don't think. I get mad one day at all gringos, and I start out. Now is too late."

His words caused her to study him. They made her feel just a little sorry for him. He was a handsome man. He was not tall, scarcely taller than she, but he had a fine physique under his worn *charro* clothes. She was surprised that he wore the Mexican garb. It made him more conspicuous than she would have thought he'd want to be.

"Why do you wear those clothes?"

"You want to see me without?"

She flushed. "I mean, you are dressed like a Mexican and —"

"Hell, I am a Mexican. I told you."

He exasperated her until she lost a little of her fear. "You know what I mean."

"I wear because I'm proud to be Mexican."

"I see."

"I glad you see. Now you understand, eh?"

"Some."

"Good! You understand first. Then maybe you like Sabás."

"Why should I?"

"Already you forget those Paiutes, eh?"

"No," she said slowly. "No, I haven't forgot what you did."

He got up and moved over to sit beside her. The meager fire had died to embers but now it suddenly flared, and they both stared into it.

"I take care of you," he said. "When they get me, then you go back to your people."

"That might be years!"

He shook his head, still looking at the dying blaze. "I think it be pretty soon. They got a big reward for me now. Some hombre, he going to get me for that money."

She was startled by what he said. "How do you know that?"

He turned to face her. "Maybe you know something, eh? Maybe you know who is looking for me now?"

"How should I know?"

"I hear they got three thousand dollars for me."

She nodded before she thought.

"You know, eh?"

"I read it in the newspapers."

"Orozco now is famous. Like Vásquez was."

"Does that make you feel good?" she said.

"One time it would. Now it don't. Now everbody, he going to want the big reward." He paused. "So I die soon, Belle. You make me happy until, eh?"

She thought of trying to escape him but discarded the thought at once. In the trackless desert he was her only means of survival.

She sat still, frozen in her uncertainty of her future. A sudden gust of wind roared past the cave mouth. It roiled the air inside so that the fire flared again. She started, every nerve jumping.

He turned toward her and smiled. "There is much wind on the desert. You get used to. Sometimes only, though." He paused and listened, as if he could hear something coming. "This wind, it be big, I think. Maybe sandstorm. We stay here, Belle, until is over. You and me."

Benteen felt it coming too and cursed it. It would obliterate the tracks he was following. Could he have hurried the pace of his obstinate pack animal, he would have. He had to keep on as long as he could, hoping to catch sight of Leslie before the dust got bad. Once he lost the trail and his visibility, he might never pick it up again. He would have to blindly search a desert he didn't know. He knew from experience what a formidable job that would be. He had been through sandstorms before, in the Territory.

Leslie was having similar thoughts, only he was losing the trail faster. As the sand began to fill the hoofprints left by Orozco and Belle, he knew it was a losing battle for him. The wind roared through the pass, lifting the desert surface and driving it into his nostrils and his eyes. He tied a neckerchief over his nose, but that did not help him to see. He looked about for some area of shelter for himself and the animals, and off to one side he could barely discern a rocky outcrop of some sort. He headed toward it.

The lee side of it was nearly perpendicular and gave a meager protection against the stinging blast of the sand. He drew his animals in close and tethered them to a heavy boulder. They huddled there together. At least they were able to breathe.

Orozco had sat quietly and made no advances, and that made her apprehension grow. Would he suddenly attack her? In a brutal and violent rape? Her mind was numbed by the thought. Finally she could no longer stand the silence between them. She said, "This cave, isn't it unusual on the desert?"

"Is not a cave. Was dug by hombres. Looking for gold or silver. A long time ago, I think."

"How can you tell?"

He gestured at the walls. "Marks of pick and shovel. Mexican prospectors, most like." He paused. "You know, Belle, Mexicans, they the first to look for gold on the desert. Maybe twenty, thirty years ago. You know who first find silver at Sierra Gorda? Hombre named Luis Fuentes. You think he is gringo? Hell no. But the gringos, they come and cheat him out. Now Mexicans at Sierra Gorda, they only work for gringos. Don't own hardly nothing."

She was silent.

His voice rose. "You understand? Like with the ranchos! The goddamn gringos, they got it all."

"I'm sorry," she said. She did not know why she said it.

"That's why I get mad one day and turn bandido." He moved closer to her. "You lonely?"

"No!"

Outside the wind tore past the open entrance to their refuge. Dust drifted in, but they were protected. The temperature had dropped.

"Desert is a crazy place," he said. "Sometimes hot as hell, sometimes *muy frío*. Worse when the wind blow." He looked at her closely. "You get lonely, Belle, you tell me, eh?"

Benteen kept on. Eyes slit, he scanned ahead, forcing his reluctant animals, trying to get as far along the trail as he could before the tracks were gone. But finally he could no longer pick them out. In the last few minutes before he quit trying, the blowing sand had thickened until visibility was down to a scant five yards. He swore at himself for his stubbornness. Now he cast about in desperation for some place to hole up until the storm was over.

His pack animal refused suddenly to budge, and he tugged viciously on its lead. He thought he glimpsed a possible protection of rocks a few feet to his right, and he kicked at his mount to drive it forward. It went only a yard or so, then balked.

Swearing again, he dismounted, gave a jerk on the reins, and stepped forward.

He stepped out into nothing.

The reins tore from his hand as he dropped into a void. He fell forever, then smashed to a stop in sand. His skull exploded with light.

When he came to, his whole body was in pain. His bones were broken, he was sure of that. He panicked. He was on his back and above him against the dust-darkened sky he could see the square outline of the vertical shaft of a mine.

How far was it up there? Thirty feet? Twenty?

What did it matter how far? He was helpless to reach it.

★ ★ ★

He passed out again from the pain and the shock. When he came back to consciousness, the sky far above had not changed. The wind roared across the opening, seeming to suck out the air from the abandoned shaft. He struggled to breathe and tried to move his aching body.

He was surprised when he could roll over and raise himself to his hands and knees. It did not seem possible that his back or arms or legs weren't broken.

Now, in the gloom of the bottom, he first noticed the rope ladder with wood rungs that dangled against the side of the shaft. It reached within a foot of the bottom.

Painfully he crawled toward the ladder, each movement a test for broken bones. He reached it and decided that, miraculously, he was still whole. He grasped for the ladder and pulled himself up rung by rung until he was standing. Dizziness struck him and he clung there until it passed.

He began to climb. As he got both feet on the first rung, the ladder swung his toes hard against the side of the shaft. The jar drove agony through him, but he hung on. He took another step up, swearing at his weakness, scared that he was losing his strength.

He tilted his head and looked up. Twenty

feet to go, and he had gone only two.

Suppose he got halfway up and the ladder broke? How many years had those ropes hung there rotting?

He willed himself to another rung.

And then the ladder did break, and he crashed and blackness overtook him once more.

The wind blew itself out sometime during the night. John Leslie dug himself out of the huddle under a blanket covered with piled sand. He had to force open his eyes, their lids were grit-filled and sore. His first concern was his horse and the burro.

Dread struck him as he saw one of the rope tethers he had tied to the rock was gone. And with it the burro. And all his provisions.

The horse was still tied, and thank God for that. But a partly filled canteen looped over the saddle horn was the limit of his water. Two spare canteens had gone with the burro.

He drank sparingly and did not dare to give water to the horse. He stretched the stiffness from his muscles, mounted, and rode at a slow walk through the pass, seeing no trail of Orozco and, worse, none of the burro. The blowing sand had wiped the desert clean like a giant eraser.

He had not gone far when he heard the cry

for help. At first he thought he was only hearing again the howl of the wind, a trick of his imagination after all those hours of unrelenting blast.

The cry came again, nearer now, and he reined up to listen. He studied the contours of the shallow escarpments on either side. Off to the right he noticed a strangeness to the heaping of sage- and greasewood-covered mounds.

He moved toward them slowly, listening but hearing nothing. He drew close and dismounted and walked the remaining feet, finding a path between two of the mounds.

He halted abruptly as the open shaft yawned in front of him. He got down on his hands and knees and peered into the dimness of the hole. There was no sound. He hallooed down into it. There was no reply.

He got up, went back to his horse, and remounted. Imagination, he thought. I'll be hearing that goddamn wind for days. He moved on down the slope of the pass.

Benteen came to again as a trickle of sand fell from above and struck his face. He remembered he had been shouting for help ever since the wind had stopped, shouting in the fear and dread and panic that had torn away his toughness. For the first time in his self-reliant life he needed help. Oh God! how he needed it. He had faced death with courage and steely calm many times, but never like this. Never death by thirst, by starvation, trapped alone in the bottom of a pit.

Then, his heart pumping with sudden hope, he heard movement above, like that of the creak of a saddle being mounted.

He tried to call out. But his throat was dry and his voice cracked and the sound did not come forth. He swallowed and tried again, but his call was weak.

Suddenly frantic, he was able to scream and his voice rose in desperation. He kept on screaming. But the sound of the horse got farther away.

Leslie continued down the pass for a quarter mile before he stopped. Off ahead he could see the High Sierras in the distance, faintly though because there was a heavy haze remaining in the air, whipped up by the storm.

He was not certain why he stopped. Partly because he had to decide how to find Orozco in that desert expanse which spread in front of him. He needed, too, to find the errant burro. Either task he now knew was almost helpless, considering his lack of water and sustenance and his ignorance of this land.

I was a fool to think that alone I could find

Orozco, he thought. I should have tried to form a posse. But then he thought, what good would it have done? No posse yet had been able to catch the wily bandit. The Mojave was the adopted habitat of Orozco, a land so fierce that even the Paiutes mostly avoided it. But in it Orozco had learned to live precariously, to make it a base for continued plundering.

And he, Leslie, had no choice now but to try. Not for the reward. For Belle. He had to somehow track Orozco down. He had to get Belle back.

He sat there in his saddle, mulling this over, and all the while something kept nagging at his mind.

Abruptly then, for no real reason, he turned his mount and rode back up the pass.

Benteen, far down in the shaft, kept screaming. The screaming sounded in his own ears like that of some hurt and frantic animal. It was hardly human, and he did not know from where it came. It sounded again and again and again, and he wondered why it never ended. Until at last he realized it came from him.

Abruptly he stopped. He was shocked at himself, sick at his own dissembling. He had lost his courage and, worse, he had lost his pride. By Christ! I will die a man, he thought.

I will lie here and die in silence. I will not cry out again.

Leslie rode back to the shaft. Again he dismounted and crawled to the edge. He shouted and listened. There was no answer from below. This goddamn Mojave Desert is driving me mad, he thought. I'm hearing voices. Having doubts. Riding all the way back because I don't know if I really heard something or not. Angry with himself, he took up a small stone and threw it down the shaft, listening to hear when it would strike bottom.

The sound he heard raised the hairs on his neck. A sound of outrage.

He was too astounded to answer at once. Then he called, "Are you hurt?"

There was no reply.

Did I hear it, or didn't I? he wondered. He picked up another rock but hesitated to throw it. He yelled. "Goddamnit! If you're down there, sing out!"

"Help!"

"I want to help. Are you hurt?"

There was a silence.

"Answer me!"

"Yeah, I'm hurt — some."

Leslie said, "The ladder hanging there, can you reach it?"

"I already did. And it broke." A pause.

"You got a rope?"

Leslie hated to say it. "No. Not long enough. I got only one short tether. My goddamn burro ran off with the other." He stared down into the gloom of the shaft, but he could not see the man down there. He knew the rope would not reach.

"How far down are you?"

"Twenty feet, maybe."

"I got only a ten-twelve foot rope."

"You see my horse and pack mule up there?"

Leslie glanced around him. "No."

The man down there made an unintelligible sound. Then his voice, desperate and pleading, came up. "Don't go away. For chrissake, don't go away. We got to think this out." A pause. "You hear me?"

"Yeah, I hear." And what the hell will that do, Leslie thought.

The voice came up again. "You, up there! You got to get me out of here."

There was a desperation in the voice that tore at Leslie's gut. He could imagine how the man down there felt, how he would feel in the same predicament. He knew the man's terror. But he did not know how to help.

"For chrissake," the man said again, "don't go away!"

"I got to look around for my goddamn

burro. Or for yours. Or your horse. I got to find another rope," Leslie yelled. He hesitated then, not leaving at once, waiting to hear how the man down there would take his words.

The words came up, less frantic now, as if the man had gained back his control. "All right. I'm trusting you to come back, you hear? You wouldn't leave a man down here" — the voice showed some panic again — "to die, would you?"

"No. I'll just take a quick look around. You hear?"

"I hear." There was some discouragement in the words, as if the man suddenly realized the hopelessness of finding a rope out in the middle of the desert.

Leslie understood. He felt the same hopelessness himself.

CHAPTER 7

Leslie rode a circle a couple of hundred yards out from the abandoned shaft. He saw no trace of his burro or the other man's animals. How was he ever going to get the man out?

As far as he could see in any direction, nothing moved. He went back to the shaft and called down, "I'm here."

"You find anything?"

Leslie hesitated, then said, "No. No sign of anything."

"You got any water?"

"Some. A half-empty canteen."

"Pull up the ladder and let it down. I need water bad."

"Isn't the ladder broke?"

"Not that far up. I can reach the end."

Leslie began hauling on the ropes. He took a short drink himself, then tied the canteen carefully to the one frayed end and lowered it slowly. He kept his hand on the ladder and he could feel the man below fumbling at the canteen.

After a long pause, the voice down there called, "Thanks."

"I'm going to pull it up again," Leslie yelled.

"Go ahead."

He hauled it up hand over hand until the ladder lay in a coiled heap beside him. His mind began to work on the problem. He walked away from the shaft, stretching the ladder out full length. Only one rope had broken, the other still extended beyond. He tied the broken ends together and shortened the other side with a bight so that the rungs were even.

He got the tether rope from his saddle and fastened one end to one of the iron rings bolted into a sun-dried, rock-hard timber that was buried just beneath the surface of the ground. Was the beam rotted? He didn't think so. He knew how wood hardened in the Arizona sun; it would be the same here.

He threaded the tether rope through the wood rungs, making a clove hitch around the center of each one. He could be adding half-again to the strength of the ladder, he believed, and his hope began to rise. But then he reached the end of the tether, and the hitches had shortened it by several feet. Only the top half of the ladder was reinforced.

The man below began to shout. Leslie went back to the edge to listen.

"What the hell you doing up there?"

Leslie tried to tell him.

"Hell, man, that ladder is rotten. I told you that."

"I got the top half strengthened."

"Goddamnit, it broke once and near killed me. I feel busted up now. Another time, and I'll be dead."

"You got to take the chance. You get past halfway and it'll be stronger," Leslie said. He was not at all sure of this.

"I'll never get past halfway. You can see the bottom part is what busted."

Leslie looked around in desperation. The horse stood with reins trailing in ground hitch. He eyed the reins. They could give a few more feet of reinforcing if he removed them from the bridle. So could the cinch and the latigos, and the thin leather jockey ties, if needed.

"Hold on!" he called down. "I got more work to do."

But now he had the problem of the horse wandering off. He solved it by using the lighter tie straps for hobbles, hoping they would hold.

He worked for nearly half an hour before he was satisfied. In that time he'd gone back once to the shaft to explain to the man below what he was doing.

"Jesus!" was all the man said.

He finally had it done and lowered the makeshift contrivance down into the hole.

There was a period of silence, then, "Jesus!" the man down there said again. But almost at once Leslie could see the ladder tauten as he tested it with his weight.

Leslie stared down into the shaft. The sky was getting lighter now as the dust cleared. He could see the man's hat come into sight then stop as the climber halted for breath.

"This son of a bitch busts now, I'm dead," the climber said.

Leslie held his breath, afraid to speak.

And then it happened. One rope broke and the climber dropped as the rungs beneath him collapsed.

Leslie's heart jumped.

The man on the ladder began to swear in fright and frustration.

Leslie could see he still had a chance. "Step up, man. Step up!"

"How, goddamnit? My foot's caught."

"Step up. Get your weight on the other one."

The climber rose a little as he did so. He began kicking his entangled foot, trying to get it loose.

"Easy!" Leslie said. "You'll kick the whole thing apart."

The hat rose again toward him. Now he

reached down as the climber came to the top rung and clawed upward. A moment later Leslie pulled him out of the shaft, and he lay stretched out, breathing hard.

It was a full minute before he rolled over and sat up and looked at his rescuer. He said simply, "Thanks. I owe my life to you." He sat there then, unable or unwilling to move, his head drooping.

Leslie felt completely drained himself.

Finally the man lifted his eyes to meet Leslie's and said, "A man stupid enough to step into a mine shaft, I reckon he deserves what he gets. But when it's your own self that done it, you get to thinking different."

"I reckon so."

"Damn dust storm. I should have known better. Stepped out blind and that was it." He stood up and held out his hand. "Name of Tom Benteen."

"Leslie, John Leslie."

Benteen let go of his hand as if it was a snake. His face went white. It showed a strange mix of emotions.

"What's wrong?"

Benteen kept staring at him. His jaw clenched and unclenched. His wide mouth pressed into a hard line.

Something was working in the man and Leslie tried to ease it. He said, "I've seen sandstorms before, but none as bad as this was."

"Where?"

"Arizona."

"I thought."

"Why do you say that?"

Benteen hesitated before he answered. "I seen them there too."

"This damned Mojave — hell, it's worse than the Territory."

Benteen was silent, then said, "Only three reasons to be out here, I'd say. One, a man works out here at mining. Two, he's out here running away. Three, he's out here hunting somebody."

"Could be."

"Which one are you?"

Leslie gave him a curious look. "A bold question, friend. Which are you?"

"I'm hunting somebody."

"Orozco?" Leslie was suddenly excited by the thought.

"Maybe."

"Me too. I was on his trail, but now there's no more tracks."

"Yeah."

Leslie sized Benteen up. "You got the look of a riding man. What did you do in the Territory?"

"Scouted for the army. Running down renegade Apaches. You out for the reward?"

"I was. Now it's more than that. The son of a bitch has got my woman with him."

"I heard."

"Where?"

"Sierra Gorda."

"Don't remember seeing you around."

"Was only there a few hours. Couple of days ago."

"I see. Listen, I need help to get my woman."

"Your woman or the reward?"

Leslie thought. Hell, he needed the reward. Or had. That had been the whole idea. But now that was nothing compared to getting her back. He said, "We could split the reward."

"Two thousand dollars, ain't it?"

"Three now, one way or another."

"I don't know." Whatever was troubling Benteen still showed in his face.

"The woman," Leslie said, "don't you have any feeling about her? Being out there in that Mex bandit's hands."

"Maybe."

"If you'd ever met Belle, you would."

"Matter of fact, I have."

Leslie was surprised. "When?"

"Stayed a day or two at her boardinghouse."

"Did you know she came up on the desert?"

"I heard all about what happened."

"Damned fool thing to do," Leslie said. "She was on the Sierra Gorda stage when he took her. Could have been on the way up to see me. I keep wondering why."

"Hard to figure a woman."

"Will you help me find her?"

Benteen was silent.

"Christ! man, you know what a fine woman she is. Don't you have any human feeling?"

Still Benteen didn't answer. He limped away from Leslie as if his entire body was bruised. He stood staring off into the hazy distance, looking at nothing at all. Finally he came limping back. He stared hard at Leslie. "You saved my life, damn you."

Leslie did not understand his tone, but he said, "I need you to track him down over this goddamn desert. I realize that now."

"Do I need you?"

Leslie's face hardened. That's gratitude for you, he thought. How long does it last? He said, "Take all of the reward. All I want is Belle." When Benteen still said nothing, he said, "What more can you want?"

"Something else."

"What?"

"I can't tell you that now. Not when you just saved my life." Benteen stared into Leslie's eyes. "But, friend, there will come a time when I'll tell you. You can be sure of that."

The words sounded strange to Leslie. Falling down that shaft, he thought, it might have affected Benteen's mind. Struck his head maybe. His body was hurt bad, you could tell that the way he walked. Still, he could likely find his way around the Mojave. He looked tough. A scout was in his proper element here. If there was any chance of tracking down Orozco, he'd be the one could do it.

"Will you help me?"

"For all of the reward?" There was a sardonic look in Benteen's eyes. "I reckon so."

Ungrateful bastard! Leslie thought, but he said, "It's yours."

Benteen nodded at the heaped rope ladder with its pieces of reinforcing. "Get your riding gear back together," he said. "First thing, we got to find my horse and the pack animals."

Leslie had to boost him up into the saddle. Benteen made no sound, but he grimaced as he threw his weight on his leg in the stirrup.

Leslie hauled himself up behind the cantle. "They might have drifted south, back the way we came from."

"You're a town man for sure."

"How do you know?"

Benteen was silent. Finally he said, "I heard your name before. At Sierra Gorda. They told me you were the marshal there, and that you'd taken to Orozco's trail."

"So I'm a town man, mostly."

"That was a southwest wind was whipping up that sand. No animal would buck it." He paused. "You ain't rightly qualified to track a man across this desert."

"I'm learning the hard way," Leslie said.

They rode down to the edge of a desert valley, and Benteen reined up. "They could be anywhere down there." His eyes swept the expanse of sage and greasewood.

"They'd go for water," Leslie said. "Look for green out there."

"You're learning," Benteen said. "Still too much haze to see, though. We'll ride on."

He turned west along the scarp which led along the north side of the El Pasos.

"Hell," Leslie said, "we're on the other side of the same range and going back."

"I'm sticking to the high ground for now." They rode a mile and halted again. Benteen kept staring across the valley toward the line of High Sierras. "Trees over there, base of the mountains."

Leslie suddenly felt oriented. "Place called Coyote Holes," he said. "I remember it. Stage stop on the Sierra Gorda run. Same road we both took down to the holdup site."

"I'd bet those hammerheads headed there.

117

The horse would follow."

"What about Orozco? And Belle?"

"First things first," Benteen said. "That's the law of the desert."

It was farther than it appeared, but eventually they rode up to the cluster of cottonwoods and shacks and stables and corral that made up the stage station. The station keeper came forth and stared at them. He was a burly, middle-aged man with a disgruntled expression, but his greeting was friendly enough. "Hell of a way to get around. Two men on a horse. You trying to save money?"

"Looking for a couple of pack mules and a blue roan," Benteen said.

"I got the bastards. Drifted in this morning after the big blow. I give them hay and water and put them in the corral back there." A pause. "You're lucky you didn't lose the one you're riding, ain't you?"

Neither answered. Ask a fool question, don't expect an answer, Leslie thought.

A little put out, the station man said, "I stripped off your gear and the packs. Got the stuff in the storeroom."

"Thanks," Leslie said.

"Didn't I see both you gents come through on the stage last few days?"

"Yeah."

"You should have bought round-trip tickets.

118

Beats doing it the hard way like you gents done. How cheap can you be?" He grinned at Benteen.

Benteen did not smile back. He said to Leslie, "Get down. I'm hurting bad and you're in my way."

Leslie slid off the horse, and Benteen swung his right leg over the cantle in one swift movement. But he groaned when his foot hit the ground. He hung there with his left foot still in the stirrup.

The station keeper stared. "You hurt, mister?"

"He fell down a mine shaft," Leslie said, and moved to ease Benteen's boot loose.

"For chrissake!" the station man said. "You two don't look like a couple of greenhorns."

"It can happen to the best of us," Leslie said. "How about something to eat?"

"Sure. Turn that poor tired beast into the corral and come on in."

The station keeper laid out a meal for them and sat down at the long table. "Name of Will Osmond," he said.

"John Leslie. And that's Tom Benteen."

"Leslie? Hell, ain't you the new marshal at Sierra Gorda?"

"Was. Not now."

"Short career," Osmond said.

"You hear any more about Orozco since he

stole that girl off the stage?" Benteen said.

"So that's it! I didn't think you gents looked like prospectors. For one thing, there wasn't no picks and shovels on them pack mules."

"You ought to be a detective," Benteen said. "Ever think of hiring out to the Pinkertons?"

"About Orozco?" Leslie said.

"Haven't heard no more. That's the way he is. Go for a couple months sometimes and don't hear a thing. Then bang, he robs a stage. Or takes a couple of silver ingots off a bullion freighter. Or goes over the Walker Pass here, west to Havilah, and robs some poor storekeeper there. Understand they upped the reward since he robbed Mr. Barker."

"Barker raised it," Leslie said. "Provided he's brought in dead."

"All for a watch," Osmond said. "It happened right here, you know. Orozco had me and the others tied up, waiting for the stage. Only one passenger that day, and the driver. Passenger was Barker. Barker asked Orozco to give his watch back, said it was a family heirloom. Orozco asked him how many family heirlooms he had robbed Mexicans of, including the San Juan mine at Sierra Gorda. Called him a bigger bandit than he, Orozco, was."

"Might be some truth to that," Leslie said.

"I never seen a man as mad as Barker was. Then Orozco held his gun on him and tossed the watch on the floor and told Barker to get down on the floor and crawl to get it if he wanted it that bad. For a minute I thought Barker was going to do it. But in the end he didn't. He just stood there staring at Orozco with hate coming out of his eyes.

"And Orozco said, 'All right, you gringo *hideputa*.' And stepped on the watch and smashed it with his boot heel."

"And added another thousand dollars on his head," Leslie said. He looked at Benteen.

Benteen was thinking. He said, "He come here often?"

"No. Not anymore. I think he's getting spooked about bounty hunters. He's gone deeper into the desert."

They ate in silence for a while, then Osmond said, "Sometimes he hits the other stage south out of the Panamints. The one that runs through Lone Willow Station and Granite Wells. That's the route to San Bernardino through the Cajon Pass."

"How far?"

"To Lone Willow? I'd guess forty miles. That pass you come through, you was a part way there."

Benteen shoved his chair back, grunting in pain as he did so. He sat then in deep thought. "That's likely where he went then. He'd not have headed east otherwise. We lost him in the pass over there."

"Rademacher."

"What?"

"Rademacher Pass. Got its name from some old Dutchman dug a hole over there."

"Goddamn his eyes!" Benteen said. "Likely the hole I fell into." He stood up. "We'll saddle up and head right back there. Should be new tracks beyond the pass maybe. We lost some time, but it makes no difference. Not in the end."

"I'm ready," Leslie said.

Osmond led them to where he'd stored their gear, then helped Leslie saddle the horses and tie the packs on the burros. Benteen stood by helplessly, so stiff now he could scarcely move.

"You going to make it?" Leslie said.

"I keep thinking about the reward."

"And you?" Osmond said to Leslie.

"I keep thinking about the woman. She's mine."

"I hope you get him," Osmond said. "On account of her."

They picked up the trail almost at once as they reached the Rademacher. The tracks were plain enough, coming down through the narrow part of the pass, then turning east instead of toward Coyote Holes.

They both stared at them.

"The son of a bitch!" Leslie said. "He came out after we did! What held him up?"

Benteen said, "You don't want me to tell you."

"The bastard!"

"Remembering Belle's looks," Benteen said, "I can understand the delay."

"They can't be far ahead."

"No. Not far. Just the time it took us to get back these critters. We push hard, we ought to catch up."

"I'm ready."

"Well, Marshal, I'm not. I'm one solid bruise all over."

"You won't go on?"

"I didn't say that. I said I wasn't ready. Not to lock horns with an hombre as tough as this Orozco is supposed to be."

"You find him and I'll do the horn locking."

"Alone?"

"I was alone before."

Benteen gave him a long, appraising stare. "You must be one hell of a hand with that six-gun," he said, nodding toward Leslie's holster. "You must have some kind of a rep to land a marshal's job at Sierra Gorda."

"There and other places."

"Such as?"

"Jericho. In the Territory."

"Jericho? Strange. I been through there."

"I don't recall you."

"I didn't stay long."

"I usually checked out strangers riding through."

"You might have been out of town."

"What would you be doing there?"

"Just riding through. And like I said, you might have been taking time off."

Leslie thought about this. It was kind of odd, he thought. In ten years he couldn't remember missing more than a half-dozen nightly rounds of the town.

CHAPTER 8

In the cave Belle awakened in Orozco's arms.

She lay still, wondering at how peacefully she had slept after he'd had his way with her. God! she thought, have I come to this? That I can lie here in a stranger's embrace without shame? A month ago, a week ago, she would never have believed it.

But he had not been rough with her. He had been a lover. A passionate seducer, not a rapist. Surprisingly, after a first protest, she had succumbed without struggle, astonishing herself. Even now she lay quiet, not yet wanting him to awaken, not yet wanting to leave his arms. She had been too long without a man, she thought. Except for that one afternoon with John Leslie.

Had Johnny aroused her long dormant desires? Or was it this physically attractive *latino* who stirred the fire?

Was it so terrible that she had not tried to fight him off ? Would he have beaten her if she had? She would never know for sure, but she did not think so. Now, the beginning of guilt disturbed her contentment.

She tried to rationalize the guilt away. After

all, she told herself, he saved me from rape or worse by those Paiutes.

She kept on lying there. He rescued me just in time, she thought. She shuddered and tried to snuggle closer.

He awoke. He squeezed her tightly, kissed her hard, then pulled himself away and stood up. He moved out of the cave with the restless grace of a great cat. Presently he came back with an armful of greasewood and threw it on the ashes of the dead fire. He drew out a match and got a fire going again.

Neither had spoken. She got up and went out to relieve herself. When she returned, he had bacon in a pan and water for coffee on the fire.

"You hungry, Belle?"

She shook her head, keeping her eyes on him. Looking at him gave her pleasure. This had not been so before.

"Sabás?"

"*Sí*, Belle?"

"What do you intend to do?"

"What you mean, Belle?"

"With me."

"With you? I'm going to do what I done last night. You don't like?"

She wanted to say no, but she couldn't.

"You don't like? Or do you?"

She flushed. "That isn't what I meant."

126

"What you mean, Belle? You speak plain English so I can understand."

"You know what I mean."

He smiled. "Sure, I know. You worried about maybe I don't treat you good. You don't got to worry, Belle. Sabás, he's in love with you. I'm a long time that I don't have a woman to love, I told you. You think I don't treat you right? You see. You my woman now."

"But you have to keep running."

"Sure. So you got to run too. All over this goddamn desert. But sometimes we stop, you and me, and make love together."

"How long can it last?"

He shrugged. "Who knows? Next month, next week. Maybe mañana. But until then, eh? You and me, Belle."

"Aren't you afraid to die?"

He turned the bacon in the pan over with a knife. Then he met her eyes. He said, "Mexicans, they ain't afraid to die. Not most, anyway."

"Why is that?"

He did not answer at once. Then he said, "I don't know. It is the way we are. Maybe because to live is *muy* hard for most Mexicans." He gestured to a sack nearby. "Get them tortillas, Belle. We going to eat now."

They ate in silence. Her mind kept running over what he had said. He had a strange philosophy, she thought. But mostly she kept thinking about what he'd said about making love. It excited her. Being on the run with a notorious bandit was exciting too. A week ago she could never have believed she would be doing that either.

Her life had been dull. There had been no excitement before or after she had married Fred Jackson. She had thought there would be. Coming to California, she'd had great expectations. Why, she could not have said. Then Fred had bought the boardinghouse, and he had hired on as a freighter, and her life had been ten years of boredom ever since.

Often she had thought back to her relationship with John Leslie and seen she had made a mistake. Her life with him would have been one of fear for his safety, but it would never have been so dull.

Suddenly the thought struck home that it was she who might be responsible if death came to Sabás. It was because of her that Johnny set out to get the reward. Suppose he was even now on their trail?

She had a sinking feeling at the thought. If Johnny killed Sabás because of her — Or if Sabás killed Johnny — Oh God! she thought, please don't let it happen.

He moved to her and embraced her again. "Belle," he said. "Belle!"

She clung to him, afraid for him, afraid for Johnny, her emotions in a turmoil of fear and desire and self-blame.

Gradually then, as his hands removed her clothing, as his kisses covered her body, only the desire was left.

They were riding stirrup to stirrup. From time to time he turned his head and met her glance and smiled.

She did not smile back.

"You not happy?" he said finally.

"Should I be?"

"Hell yes! Back there in the cave you happy, no?"

She blushed. He had a way of talking that made her feel half-ashamed.

"You worry about me?" he said.

"Yes. That's part of it."

"Hell, I ain't going to hurt you, Belle."

"It's something else."

"You going to tell me or no?"

"There is a man on your trail."

He shrugged. "It happens a lot of times."

"He is good with a gun." She held up her hand, thumb up, two fingers pointing at him. "With a revolver."

"Ah! a *pistolero*. How you know this?"

"I can't tell you that."

He shrugged again. "It's all right. I kill him.

You don't worry."

"No!"

"What you mean, no?"

"He's a — he's a friend of mine."

"Too bad. He no is friend of mine."

"I shouldn't have told you."

"Why not? You want he should kill me?"

"No!"

He grinned. "Hell, woman, you got to make up your mind. Him or me?"

"I don't want either of you to die."

He gave her a closer look, his eyes narrowed. "You don't tell me everything. This hombre, you in love with him too?"

"Yes."

"Hell, how you can love him and me both?" He grinned again.

She was angry at his grinning. "I don't. *He* is the man I am going to marry."

"You going to have to wait, I think," he said. "He's after the money, eh? Well, he got to catch me first." He paused. "He going to use the reward money to marry you, Belle? You want that?"

"No!"

"Well, I don't think he going to get that reward. So then you only got Orozco to love."

"You're insane."

"Insane?"

"Crazy."

"Ah, *loco*. Sure, I'm loco. You got to be loco to be a bandido."

"It's my fault."

"No, Belle. I'm loco before I meet you."

"I mean it's my fault he's hunting you. Oh, I wish I could explain it to you."

"You try and I understand. I'm loco, not *estúpido*."

She hesitated, then began to tell him about John Leslie, about their plan to pay off the bank with his blood money.

When she had finished, he said, "I'm sorry if I got to kill him. But maybe he don't find me. This desert, it's *muy grande*."

"Oh, I hope he doesn't! Not now."

"But if he does, Belle, one of us got to die."

She couldn't bring herself to accept that. Not when it was because of her that it would happen.

"You like to dance, Belle?"

She was startled out of her disturbing thoughts.

"Out here?"

He laughed. "Sure, why not? Any place. But no, I mean real dance. Like fandango. I used to like very much." He paused. "That's where my trouble begin. At a fandango in Los Angeles. Was first time I shoot a gringo. He insult my *muchacha* I'm dancing with. I don't like. He pull a *pistola*. We fight. The gun go off. He got shot with his own *pistola*. The sheriff he arrest *me*. I get away, come to the desert for the first time. Vásquez, he out here then, and he teach me the bandido business. Now I never go back. Hell, pretty soon I die. Pretty soon some gringo he kill me. Maybe your *pistolero*, eh?"

"Please —"

He smiled. "So. You like Sabás pretty good, eh? And Sabás, he like pretty woman like you. We make a good *pareja*, a good pair, Belle. Only for a while. Every day my life getting shorter. Well, what the hell, eh?"

"Don't talk like that."

"Why not? I make you sad?"

She nodded slowly. "Very sad." Impulsively she reached over and touched his arm. She kept wanting to touch him. God, he was a handsome son of a bitch, she thought. And if it hadn't been for him, the Paiutes —

"How long since you be married, Belle?"

"Three years."

"No good. You could give some hombre much pleasure all them years."

"Like you?"

"Sure, like me. Too bad I don't know you then. Maybe I don't get to be a bandido if I know you. Maybe I just work all day for some goddamn gringo, and you and me, we make love all night. You like?"

She wouldn't let herself answer that.

He laughed. "You like. I *know* you like. You got hot blood for a gringa."

Leslie held the crude map drawn for them by the station keeper at Coyote Holes. He said, "He's heading for Lone Willow, all right. I'd bet on it."

Benteen rode close and held out his hand. "Let's see." He studied the scrawled lines made by Osmond. "There's some hills up there ahead. But I guess you're right. He wouldn't go for Granite Wells. Not now. Too far south."

"My way of thinking. Anyhow, as long as you can pick out his tracks, we got to be going right."

They rode a while without speaking, Benteen with his own thoughts. "You were a lawman. You ever been a bounty hunter before?"

"Never have."

"Me neither. I'm wondering why you took it up this time?"

"Was the big reward in the beginning," Leslie said. "Now it's Belle."

"One thing leads to another, don't it?"

"It sure as hell does."

Benteen handed back the map. "I never had much use for bounty men. Kind of like scalp-hunters, my way of thinking."

"My way too."

"So why now?"

"Belle. She needs money to save a bank foreclosure."

"So you were going to be the big man and get it for her."

"I got one thought now. To get Belle."

"Must be an old friend."

"More than that. And it goes a long way back."

"Mighty pretty woman."

Leslie said, "How come you to give up scouting for the army?"

"How come you to give up wearing a star at Jericho?"

"I had my reasons."

"Same here."

After a silence Leslie said, "It was on account of a damn fool kid."

Benteen said nothing.

"A damn fool kid trying to make a gun rep in a hurry."

Benteen turned a hard face toward him. "You that famous in the Territory? I heard of a Hickok at Abilene, and somebody named Earp, but I never heard of you."

"I wasn't famous. But that fool kid must have got it in his head that I was."

"Tell me about it," Benteen said.

"He threw down on me while I was crossing the street. Come out of a saloon, drunker than a hoot owl, but I didn't know it then. Even so, I tried to wing him."

"And?"

"I missed and caught him in the belly. Made me sick."

Benteen said coldly, "Made him a damn sight sicker, I reckon."

"Wasn't my intention."

"Piss-poor shooting, I'd say."

Leslie shrugged. "I can't argue that. Was the reason I quit and come out to Los Angeles. Figured to get into another line of work."

"And ended up where you started."

"Not quite. That's why I need your help."

"Poor damn kid," Benteen said. "He have any kin?"

"I didn't know of any."

"Did you try to find out?"

"Damn kid put two bullets into me. I didn't feel much like taking on that kind of chore."

"You ever think he might have kin come looking for you?"

Leslie looked surprised. "What for? I told you how it happened."

"That might not be enough. Not for a man's kin."

"Why not? It was pure self-defense. Anybody in Jericho would tell you that."

"You sure of that? People sometimes see things in different ways."

"Christ!" Leslie said. "I'm damn glad you ain't that kid's kin."

"Yeah. Be hell for you if I was, wouldn't it?"

"Well, you'd still have to consider I pulled you out of that shaft."

"Yeah," Benteen said. "I'd remember that. But it wouldn't be enough."

He was insatiable, Belle thought. Was it going to be like this with him to the end? No man needed so much. It had to be something in his mind that drove him. A driving desire to savor all the pleasure he could before his day of reckoning came.

She could not accept his fatalistic view that his life would soon end. He was so young and so virile. He had a lust for life that contradicted his resignation. She simply could not understand him.

She could not understand her feeling toward him either. It had grown too strong, too fast. A few short days ago he had been only a name to her. Now he was her life. She could not bear the thought that Johnny might hunt him down. She was aroused at the thought. I will fight to save him, she thought. I will not let anybody kill him. I will not let even Johnny do that.

Now as she lay beside him in the shade of a steep hillock as barren as the flatland surrounding it, she thought, I have become his whore. And was not disturbed by the thought.

He had been staring at the sky, and then he turned his face to see her watching him.

"*Ojos morenos,*" he said. "Dark eyes. I'm glad you got. Is too many blue eyes here now. Too many goddamn blue-eyes gringos. Those *yanquis,* they keep coming and they take everything from us. Those goddamn blue eyes, they come to stare down the sun in old California."

"You can't fight them, Sabás."

"You wrong. I can fight. Maybe I can't beat, but I can fight. For a little while longer, Belle."

"I wish that you would not keep saying that."

"That I fight?"

"No. About only a little while longer."

"But I know is true."

"You don't have to say it."

He showed his white teeth. "All right, Belle. I don't say it no more." He paused. "But it true."

"Stop it!"

He laughed. "All right, Belle. Now you begin tell me what to do. Now you begin sound like a wife."

She wasn't sure she disliked that thought. But she was saddened by it.

She was suddenly hungry. "Can we eat?"

He stood up, pulled his trousers on, and buckled his gun belt. "There is no food."

"No food? But we left some in the cave."

"Sure. I leave for so when I need."

"There is none at all?"

"No. But we get some pretty soon. When we get to Lone Willow. The station hombre, he got plenty there."

"He will sell to you?"

He grinned and touched the butt of his Colt, worn high on his hip, vaquero-style. "Sure he sell — if I ask him right."

"Do you have to use that?"

"You got money?"

She shook her head. "The Indians, they threw my purse away."

"No matter. I ask the station hombre right."

"You'd rob him?"

"Hell, I'm a bandido, Belle. What you think?"

"What if he fights?"

He stopped grinning. "They don't many times fight Orozco. Not no more."

"You have shot men? Killed?"

He held her eyes calmly. "Belle, you don't want that I answer this thing."

She knew that was true.

He brought up the horses. "So now we ride," he said.

They did not ride up to the station. They halted a short distance away, hidden by one of the hilly outcrops that here and there broke up the monotony of the desert flats. During their approach they had skirted the south side of a dry lake and taken to a stage road there.

Belle began to worry as soon as they neared the signs of habitation. Everything seemed suddenly different now. When they were alone in the empty desert, there had been only she and Sabás and their mutual wants to consider. Now, abruptly, there were other beings intruding or being intruded upon. A kind of idyll was ending. She felt it, and she did not want it to be so.

"You wait," he said. "I go talk with the hombre."

"Sabás?"

"*Sí?*"

"Please don't shoot. Promise?"

Instead of answering, he sat his saddle, looking at her for a long time. He had an expression she had never seen before.

"Sabás?"

"Sure, Belle. Anything you want. I ask the

hombre nice. I be polite. You no worry, eh?"

"Please, Sabás."

"Sure, Belle. I do like you say." He slid his carbine out of its saddle scabbard and handed it to her. He turned abruptly away and rode toward the willow that gave the station its name. He kept his eyes on where he was going. He did not look back. Only then did she realize he still had the gun on his hip.

He neared the station and became hidden among the outbuildings. Minutes passed and tension held her motionless beside the horses. She still held the carbine in her grasp.

Then she saw him ride back into sight, a large cloth sack bulging with goods slung in front of him.

He came toward her, not looking back, and she guessed he had tied up the station keeper and anybody else who was there. He waved a hand at her, and even at that distance she could see his smile.

She said aloud, "Thank God!"

And a gun blasted from the nearest building. He grabbed at his left shoulder and fell out of his saddle. The gun blasted again and kicked up sand a foot from his head.

She saw smoke float from the entrance of the outbuilding, and without thought she raised the carbine, levered in a cartridge, and shot at it blindly. There was a scream, and a man fell out through the doorway and did not move.

She got on her horse and raced it toward where Sabás lay.

CHAPTER 9

He was bleeding badly. But he had managed to get back in the saddle by the time she reached his side. His face was pale beneath his olive skin.

"You got to help me, Belle," he said.

She threw a glance over to where the man she'd shot lay in the yard. He was still clutching a revolver, and he was starting to stir.

Thank God, she thought, I didn't kill him.

And then he opened fire with the gun, and she began to wish she had.

The shooting stopped abruptly, and when she looked again the man was lying facedown in the dirt, his gun hand extended but still.

Oh God! she thought. Don't let him die!

Sabás spurred his horse to a run, and she followed. They reached the spare mounts and she fastened the leads.

"I've got to look at your wound."

His face was set with pain. "Pretty soon, Belle. I got a place, maybe ten miles."

"Will they find us?"

"No. Take a damn good tracker to find us. Them station hombres I tie up, they don't going to find no trail at all." He paused. "Anyhow, we got food now. You still hungry, Belle?"

She thought about the man she had shot. She shuddered. She didn't think she'd ever be able to eat again. She was an accomplice to armed robbery now. She might be a murderer too. She halted suddenly and slipped from her saddle. She stood clutching the reins and retched.

Leslie and Benteen rode into Lone Willow and found the station keeper and two of his employees still tied, and the other lying in the yard with a bullet through his thigh. He was in bad shape from exposure, loss of blood and shock. They carried him into his sleeping quarters, cleaned, and bandaged his wound.

"What happened here?" Leslie said as they worked.

The station keeper gave his description of the action up until the time Orozco had left three of them bound inside the place.

"What about him?" Benteen said. He nodded toward the wounded man.

"Louie? Hell, I don't know. Orozco shot him, I reckon."

Louie seemed to come out of his shock as he heard his name. He was a youngish man, hardly more than a boy. He reminded Leslie slightly of the Bodie Kid. Louie said weakly,

"Wasn't Orozco . . . I shot *him* out of his saddle."

"Who then?" the station agent said.

"A woman . . . I think. I fell outside . . . When I looked up, a woman was riding in to help him . . . I emptied my gun, but I didn't hit nothing . . . The last I seen, they was riding away together. . . ."

Leslie's skin crawled. It had to be Belle! Desperately he said, "A Mexican woman?"

"No . . . white."

Benteen said, "Well, well, think of that."

"There's got to be a reason," Leslie said.

"Sure. And you and I both know what."

"You got no right to say that!"

Benteen met Leslie's eyes. "No? Then what's your thought on it?"

Leslie did not answer. His own thought was too much the same.

"You better hope this kid don't die," Benteen said. "Seems like you and your woman are both hell on kids."

"It had to be an accident."

"She'd have a hell of a time convincing a jury of that. Or vigilantes either."

"Vigilantes?"

"Why not? We bring Orozco in, there'll be a lot of hollering for a quick hanging. Hell, you're a lawman, you ought to know that. And that hanging could include your woman."

Leslie had seen his share of lynch mobs. He knew that what Benteen had said was true. He began to wish now that he had never got into this thing of hunting down a man for bounty. It had always gone against his grain, and now it was getting worse.

But now it wasn't Orozco he was after, it was Belle. He had to get her out of the outlaw's hands before she got into deeper trouble. Although if the kid, Louie, died, she was in about as deep as she could get. What the hell was she thinking of? Why fight to protect Orozco? Why didn't she run away when Orozco was shot?

Benteen's snide comment about this came to him again. He tried to ignore it, but he couldn't. The implication was more than he could bear. No! he wouldn't let himself believe she had become Orozco's woman.

Benteen had deliberately stirred him up, talking about the possibility of the kid dying. Louie had lost blood and suffered from exposure, but the bullet had gone through his thigh without hitting bone or artery. Chances were he'd be up and around before long.

What was Benteen trying to do to him? Why did he bring up the killing in Jericho again? For a man who was obliged to Leslie for saving his life, he had a strange manner of showing his gratitude.

★ ★ ★

Orozco's head was down. Time after time he had jerked himself upright, only to slump again in his saddle. Belle rode as close to him as she could, fearful that he might tumble off his horse. But somehow he managed to hang on, clinging to the saddle horn, while she kept them on the dusty stage road north.

He had not spoken for many miles, when suddenly he straightened and said, "We turn west now, Belle. I got a place in them mountains."

She turned as he indicated. Presently she looked behind them and saw the hoofprints they were leaving. She said, "We could be followed."

"I don't can ride much more. I think we lose them in the hills."

"Them?"

"If anybody they following. Maybe them station hombres they got loose now."

"How much farther?"

"Pretty soon. We be all right, Belle. I think them station hombres they don't be good for trailing."

She didn't have the heart to tell him that maybe John Leslie could. Still, Johnny was a townsman mostly. Probably he wasn't much better than the station men at reading sign. The thought gave her hope.

146

Sabás, by what effort of will, remained upright now and led the way into the lower reaches of another barren range of mountains. His eyes kept studying ahead, as if he were picking the way. There was no trail apparent to Belle.

He halted suddenly and stared at the ground in front of them.

"What is it?"

"Look there."

She rode closer and saw the other hoofprints that angled in from the right. She didn't know what to make of them.

He sat a long time in silence, studying them. Finally he said, "Well, we got to go on."

"Who is it?"

"I don't know. Somebody, I think, he knows my place in them mountains. Maybe he knows there is spring there. We got to take a chance, Belle. We got to see who is there."

"It could be an enemy."

"Maybe." He puts heels to his horse. "We going to find out."

She was worried, but she followed.

They entered a narrow canyon. There was a sharp bend in it, and he stopped again. They could smell the smoke of a campfire on the air.

"Whoever is," he said, "he don't worry about nothing." He paused. "There only one crazy bastard like that roaming around."

"Who?"

He didn't answer. Instead he began riding forward again.

"*Alto!*"

"*Cómo no!*" Orozco said. "Of course!"

A Mexican holding a rifle came from around the bend. He was big for his race, with dark skin and Indian features. He, like Orozco, wore *charro* clothes. He stared expressionlessly at them. "Is you, Sabás?"

"Hell no, it ain't me. Is somebody else."

"Amigo!"

"*Cómo te ha ido?* How has it gone with you, Lázaro?"

"*Muy bien,* amigo." Lázaro Nuñez peered closely. "You have much blood. A bad wound, eh? Come, amigo, we got to fix you up." His eyes swept to Belle. "You his woman, eh? So come on, he don't look good to me."

They moved deeper into the canyon and came to the fire.

Nuñez went to the side of Orozco's horse and helped Orozco down. "Goddamn, man, you hurt bad." He kept speaking English, and Belle had the feeling this was for her benefit, as if he wanted her to know he knew the language. There was something strange about that, she thought.

But she dismounted and moved over to help

him lay Sabás down.

He brushed his big arm against hers as they bent over the wounded man. He turned his head and, for the first time, he smiled. He had big yellowish teeth. Not at all like Orozco's.

He was an ugly man by any standards. She was afraid of him on his appearance alone.

He got Orozco's jacket off and his shirt. He pulled a filthy handkerchief from his pocket and wiped at the blood.

"Wait!" She spoke in outrage, forgetting her fear. "Don't you have any water?"

"Sure." He pronounced it "chure." He waved at a canteen sitting nearby.

She said, "Let me," and got the canteen. She took a reasonably clean handkerchief from her clothing and poured water on it and began to wash around the wound.

Presently they could see the bluish hole where the bullet had gone in. She went to work on the back and the hole was bigger, jagged with shredded flesh.

"No es malo," he said. "No is bad."

"Do you know how to treat wounds?"

"Chure. The bullet come out, no? Just let him alone."

His casualness angered her. "Have you ever been shot?"

"Chure. Hell, I'm bandido, just like Sabás.

One time we ride together with Vásquez. We old amigos." He paused. "How he get shot?"

She told him.

He gave her a studied look. "What happened that hombre that shot him?"

"*I* shot him."

"So. You really his woman, eh? Sabás, he always good with *muchachas*."

It wasn't something she was particularly pleased to hear.

"But always they been Mexican women," he said. "Where he find you?"

Orozco, who had seemed not alert enough to hear, said, "How you know she don't find *me?*"

Nuñez laughed. "Same old Sabás. Good with *mujeres* like you no can believe. What I told you, eh, gringa?"

"Her name is Belle."

"Bell?"

"Belle."

"Ding-dong, ding-dong?"

"No. *Bella.*"

"Ah! *Sí. Muy buen* name for this one, Sabás. Goddamn! she look good to me."

"Is mine."

"Chure, is yours. But don't you going to share with your old compadre?"

"No. I don't going to share."

"Is like that, eh?" Nuñez looked his disappointment. "Well, we see. We see." He pushed roughly at the swollen flesh around Orozco's wound. "But, hombre, you in bad condition to fight Lázaro, no?"

Orozco's jaw tightened, but he said nothing.

Belle's fear of Nuñez grew. She drew away from him, not wanting to feel again the touch of his gross body. But she said, "Aren't you his friend?"

"Chure. We old friends, I told you." He showed his yellow teeth again. "But you and me, we *new* friends, eh? You like?"

She was afraid to answer him.

Orozco said. "You always got a big mouth, compadre. Even before. Now is worse. Fix me up a bandage, and shut up, eh?"

Nuñez scowled. But he said, "Chure, I fix you up right, amigo. First we got to stop the fever." He went over to his pile of gear and extracted a bottle and came back to where Orozco sat. Orozco reached out for the bottle.

"Is not to drink," Nuñez said. He shoved the mouth of the bottle against the bullet wound and held it tilted so the liquid ran into the hole.

Orozco flinched under the fiery sting, and Nuñez laughed. "Hey, hombre, you got to show your woman how *bravo* you are."

"What are you doing!" Belle said.

"Is *aguardiente*. You call brandy."

"Give me to drink," Orozco said. "God-damn! that hurt."

"One time more, compadre. On the back side." Nuñez shoved him roughly forward and did the same thing again. He looked like he was enjoying Orozco's pain.

"Christ!" Orozco said. "Give me to drink, Lázaro."

Nuñez handed him the bottle, and Sabás took a good pull at it.

"I like your woman," Nuñez said.

Orozco drank again of the *aguardiente*. He said, "You touch her, I kill you."

Nuñez was grinning now. He reached suddenly and removed Orozco's gun from his holster. "Is like that, eh? Well, I better don't take chances."

Orozco had grabbed at his hand and missed. He said, "Amigo, you don't got to do that. You don't touch Belle, we don't have no trouble."

"Chure. So like I told you, I better don't take no chances."

Benteen's sharp eye picked up the place where Orozco and Belle had left the roadway. Leslie knew he would likely have missed it. Once again he was glad he had Benteen with him, even though he had bargained away the reward money, to make certain of his help.

He would never have kept this far on Orozco's trail without it.

"He's heading for a spot to hole up, I'd guess," Benteen said. "That wound must be bothering him."

"We got to be careful if there's shooting. We got to think of Belle."

"Well, we got the advantage. Two against one." Benteen looked at Leslie. "Or do you reckon she'd side with him now against us?"

"Christ no!"

"She shot that kid back there to save him. You forgetting that?"

"I wish I could."

"Well?"

"She's going to marry me."

"You ain't sure of that. Not now. The way she acted at Lone Willow, I wouldn't put all my chips on that."

"What the hell happened?" Leslie said. "I can't understand what the hell happened."

"You don't want to understand," Benteen said.

Leslie was silent.

Benteen said, "We're lucky that there's only him and the girl. It'd be tougher if he wasn't a lone wolf."

They sat eating the meal that Nuñez had ordered Belle to prepare for them. Orozco sat propped against a rock, weak from what he had gone through.

Nuñez said, "Sabás, I been make you very famous."

"What you mean?"

"Every place I rob, I tell them I am Sabás Orozco. Some joke, eh?"

"I don't like that too much," Orozco said.

"Hell, hombre, I been make you more famous than Vásquez been."

"You kill anybody lately?"

"Have you?"

"No."

"You see? Without what I done, nobody going to be scared of Orozco."

"You kill then?"

"Chure," Nuñez said. "I kill three day ago. Couple of gringo miners near Sierra Gorda. But I give you credit for that too. Big joke, eh?"

"You damn fool!" Orozco said. "They going to make the reward for me bigger and bigger."

"Chure." Nuñez laughed. "That is what make it funny, Sabás. Better you than me."

"I don't think so."

"Ay, hombre, they going get us both pretty soon, we don't leave this place. Me, I am think to go to Arizona. They don't bother Lázaro Nuñez there. Me, I ain't famous like Sabás

154

Orozco. I ain't two places at one time, like him."

"Why you kill them miners at Sierra Gorda?"

"I do it for fun. And it make a better joke on you, amigo. They want you for murder now. Before, maybe only for robbing."

Belle felt her anger growing. She said to Sabás, "Have you killed?"

He hesitated. "Maybe sometimes in gunfights to get away. Maybe I kill, maybe not. I don't kill nobody in cold blood, like Lázaro."

His words disturbed her more than those of Nuñez. She had not let herself think about the crimes Sabás had committed. She had kept such thoughts out of her mind. Now suddenly she was confronted by them, and she was taken by a feeling of shock and despair.

And she was reminded that she had just shot a man herself. She turned cold at the thought.

Nuñez looked at her. He said, "Maybe you killed that hombre too, eh, gringa?"

"Oh God! I hope not."

"You stay with Lázaro. You get so you like."

Orozco stiffened. "I told you no!"

"I keep forget. Anyhow, what you going do about it, compadre? You want to fight your good friend Lázaro over this *mujer?* Hell, you ain't big enough, even without a wound. You want to fight with *pistolas?* Hell, you don't

155

got none — I already take away." He paused. "I think maybe I have some fun with this gringa right now. You rest, Sabás. You watch. I do all the work, eh?"

"Bastardo!"

Nuñez reached over and grabbed Belle and jerked her into his powerful arms. He mashed his whiskery mouth against hers, hugging her cruelly so she could barely breathe. From the corner of his eye he watched Orozco.

Orozco slid a hand into his boot and came out with a derringer. He fired a shot that grazed the back of Nuñez's neck.

Nuñez whirled Belle around so she was between them. He held her with one arm and pulled out his revolver and pointed it at Orozco. "All right, amigo. I guess you got to die. Too bad you don't share with your compadre." He pulled the trigger.

Belle, hearing his words, gave a convulsive jerk that spoiled his shot.

And a rifle spat from the canyon bend and kicked up gravel into Nuñez's face, blinding him.

He cried out, panicked, "Don't shoot, Sabás! We got to fight together!"

It was Leslie's shot that had blinded Nuñez. He'd fired instinctively as he saw Belle held in the cross fire between the two Mexicans, but he had fired off target for fear of hitting her as she struggled against the embrace of the big one.

Benteen swore. "Lost our surprise," he said.

Leslie ignored him. Both Mexicans had dove for the cover of the nearby rocks, the big one still clutching Belle's arm. He dragged her down harshly, and Leslie saw her strike her head as she fell.

It was Leslie's turn to swear.

Behind the rocks Nuñez still held Belle so she lay between him and Orozco. He was rubbing at his eyes, then stopped as he realized he was worsening them. He called, "Ay, Sabás, we got to fight them together."

"Maybe."

"No maybe. For true, amigo. How many you see?"

"I seen two. I don't see none now."

"Gringos?"

"I think yes."

"You and me, Sabás. Like old time, eh?" Nuñez was blinking his eyes, trying to clear them.

Orozco could see Belle lying still. "What you do with my woman?"

"She hit her head, I think."

"She still breathe?"

"Chure. She going be all right, Sabás. Don't worry."

"And after we fight these gringos?"

"Hell, I only make joke, compadre. You know I like make joke."

"I don't think so. I don't think we amigos no more, Lázaro."

Nuñez's eyes had partly cleared, and he raised himself slightly to better look at Orozco. A bullet ricocheted off the rock in front of him, and he jerked his head down. "First we fight these gringos, Sabás. All right? Then we talk about the *mujer*. Hell, hombre, she is your woman. I tell you I make joke. Hell, I'm going to Arizona. What I'm want with your woman, eh?"

He got his eyes fully cleared then and saw that Sabás had his derringer aimed directly at his head.

CHAPTER 10

"Compadre, no!" Nuñez said.

Orozco saw that Nuñez had dropped his gun during the action. "Tell me why no."

"Out there. You seen two hombres. Gringos, Sabás, gringos. You want to fight two gringos alone?"

Orozco hesitated.

"Without me, you going to die, Sabás. Think about that, eh?"

"Give to me my gun then."

Nuñez found it on the ground and, careful not to palm it, tossed it to Orozco. "You and me, Sabás. Like old times. We going to kill them goddamn gringos."

Belle began to move. She sat up. Her fine hair, loose in the sunlight, could have been a target, but no shots came from the canyon bend.

"They know about the woman," Nuñez said. "They don't going to shoot much when we got her."

Orozco had found a place to sit against another boulder. He leaned back weakly. His face was very white.

He said, "Get down, Belle. Them goddamn gringos, maybe they kill you because you shoot that hombre at Lone Willow."

She heard and understood and lowered her head. If they were men from the stage station, she would be just another bandit to them. They would be doubly bitter because she had shot one of their own. She still did not understand how she had done such a thing, except that she was trying to protect Sabás from being killed there in the stage yard. And Sabás had become her lover. She couldn't really understand that either. She only knew that it was so. God help me, she thought, what have I become?

Nuñez was speaking to her. "Hey, gringa. You good with a rifle, eh? You crawl over and get that carbine." He motioned toward his saddle gear, which was close to where Orozco was.

Would I shoot back, she thought, if the men from Lone Willow tried to kill me? She did not move.

"You want to die, gringa?" Nuñez said. "Don't you know nothing? You one of us now." He scowled. "Get the carbine."

She crawled, blankly obeying, and got the weapon.

"Is more better," Nuñez said. "Now we got three against them goddamn gringos. Don't forget, *muchacha,* you got to kill them or they kill you."

She could not believe it was happening.

"Maybe they don't know she shoot that hombre," Orozco said.

"Maybe. But maybe they do," Nuñez said.

His words didn't make her feel any better.

"That's Belle with them," Benteen said. "Bullets get to flying, she's in big danger."

"I'm thinking the same," Leslie said. "But we got to get her loose."

"Me, I'm thinking most about that reward money."

"Only that?"

"What else? She never slept with me."

"A hell of a thing to say."

Benteen nodded. "Sorry. I take it back. She seemed like a fine woman, the couple days I knew her. She comes first in this for me, same as you."

Leslie was silent. Finally he said, "There's one way might work. I'll climb my way around to the heights in back of them."

"A cross fire won't do it if Belle gets in the way."

"You got a better idea?"

"Reckon not."

"All right then," Leslie said. "I'm going to give it a try."

"What are you going to do?" Belle said.

"We wait," Nuñez said. "Hell, we got the spring. Maybe they run out of water, have to leave." He kept looking above them at the cliffs on either side and behind. "Only one thing bad this place, it don't got but only one way out."

"Then why did you choose it?" Belle said. She was frightened and angry now. She did not want to die.

"Same like Sabás," Nuñez said. "In the desert, gringa, you got to go where the water is."

"And now?"

"You and Sabás, you watch the hombre in front. Me, I watch up there." He gestured toward the cliffs. "I need the *carabina* you got. You trade me for my *pistola*."

"I've never shot a pistol."

"You never shot a *carabina* much neither, no? But you kill that man maybe at Lone Willow anyhow."

They exchanged weapons. The revolver was heavy in her hand. He grinned at her as their hands touched. His grin turned into a leer. "You and me, we going be friends, eh?"

She looked at his teeth, and she thought of the fangs of a wolf. One blast of the handgun and she could rid herself of his threat. The thought sickened her, and she let the gun drop. She could not stand to have more blood on her hands.

Unless she had to shed it to save Sabás. She'd do it then. She would not see him hang.

The thought came to her suddenly that possibly the men out there were not from the stage station. That perhaps one of them was John Leslie. The thought startled her.

Would he have learned of her abduction? If he had, he would have set out to find her, she was sure of that. She was not sure, though, if this gave her hope or not. She was becoming more and more confused by the pull of her emotions. Her life had changed in a matter of days. It all seemed so strange to her now. She wondered if she might be going mad.

"I seen a hombre up there," Nuñez said. He was crouched behind cover, his eyes on the high ground above the blind canyon.

"Where?" Belle said. She looked and saw nothing.

"Is gone now. Pretty soon he going to start shooting." Nuñez turned to Orozco. "Hey, compadre, you think you can ride?"

"Do I got to?"

"You still got a horse saddled."

"Why I want to ride?"

"You ride out of canyon, shooting. I'm going get that hombre up in the sky there."

Belle said, "No! You'll get Sabás killed!"

163

"Goddamn," Nuñez said, "you gringas got a big mouth. Is not for you to decide. Us hombres, we going decide."

"Don't go, Sabás," Belle said. "Please?"

"Maybe our best chance, Belle."

"Don't leave me alone with *him*." She moved her head toward Nuñez.

Nuñez kept his eyes on the canyon rim. "I don't bother her none, Sabás. Before I just joking. Now we got to fight a way out. You in front, amigo. Me, I get that hombre in the sky when he try to shoot you."

"What about the hombre in front?"

"You shoot him, Sabás. I got much faith in you."

At that moment they heard the man above them call out. "Belle! It's me, John Leslie!" For an instant he was exposed as he tried to make himself heard.

Nuñez sent a shot that whined off the rim to the right. He levered the carbine and squeezed off another as Belle threw herself at him, spoiling his aim.

He backhanded her across the mouth and sent her sprawling. "Goddamn gringa!"

Sabás fired his revolver and tore a hole in Nuñez's sombrero. "You hit her again, I kill you," he said.

"I would have got that hombre up there."

Sabás kept his stare on Nuñez, but he said

to Belle, "Why you do that? That hombre, he know you?"

"Yes. He is — a friend."

"He is your hombre?"

She was afraid to answer.

"So!" Sabás looked at her now. "I'm sorry, Belle. We got to kill him."

Her face hardened. "It is over between us then. I mean it."

Nuñez laughed. "You got a big problem now, Sabás."

Sabás was thoughtful. "I ride out, like Lázaro says. Maybe Lázaro he don't got to kill your hombre, Belle."

"Chure," Lázaro said.

"But then you'll get killed," Belle said.

"Maybe not. Not if you ride with me. That other hombre he must be an amigo of your hombre. He damn sure don't going to shoot you. You and me, we ride together fast. Maybe we get out with no shooting."

Nuñez said, "You take her with you, she going to ride away from you, Sabás."

"No, she don't do that. I know."

"You think you know the *mujeres*," Nuñez said. "But you forget something. This one is a gringa."

Orozco ignored this and got to his feet, grunting slightly. The horses were still sheltered from the fire of the man at the canyon bend, and he moved toward them. "Come on, Belle. Maybe we get away. Maybe your man he kill this goddamn compadre of mine too."

"I just got another more better idea, Sabás," Nuñez said. "We all going to rush that hombre in front." He handed the carbine to Orozco. "You don't let that hombre up there shoot. I get my horse saddled."

Belle looked above to where Leslie was hidden. She wondered that he did not try to shoot Nuñez. He must be afraid for me, she thought. Afraid I might get hit.

They made their rush together, Lázaro Nuñez driving the spare animals ahead of them, Orozco just behind, a lead rope tied from his saddle to the bridle of Belle's horse. Belle's ankles were lashed beneath the horse's belly. Nuñez had insisted on this to prevent her possible defection.

Benteen heard them coming and was waiting with rifle ready. He peered around the sharp bend and was momentarily confused by the dust and commotion raised by the driven spares.

He caught sight of the big Mexican through the dust and raised his weapon, and Nuñez, six-gun blasting, knocked it half out of his hands with a freak shot.

Before he could aim again they were abreast of him, both Mexicans blasting away. In the roiling dust, Benteen glimpsed the woman and was afraid to fire.

They went by him in a barrage of missed shots, and once more Belle's presence held him back. He swore out his frustration as they made their escape into the desert.

"Damn fool idea you had, climbing up behind them," Benteen said. "It gave them a way out." He waited angrily for Leslie to descend from the heights.

"I drove them right into your arms," Leslie said. "What the hell happened?"

"Fluke shot by that big greaser. That and the girl was in the way."

"You can't blame *me* for that."

"Maybe. But I ain't taking the blame either."

"I ain't giving it. Let's get after them."

"We'd best water our horses at that spring in there first. No telling where we'll find another."

"We're wasting time talking," Leslie said.

"Impatient bastard, ain't you?"

"I got reason to be."

"Let me tell you about the desert," Benteen said. "Impatience out here can kill you."

"Belle's out there with two of those bastards now. That's what I'm thinking of."

"Yeah," Benteen said. "I been thinking

about that some myself."

Leslie gave him a curious stare. How well, really, did Benteen get to know Belle in the short time she had boarded him, he wondered? A tinge of jealousy touched him, and he shook it off. If Benteen's feelings prodded him hard to get Belle away from those two that had her, he'd better be glad of it.

Lázaro Nuñez's killing of the two miners near Sierra Gorda was more than the town could tolerate. Even Barker was further aroused. He sent new demands down from the mountain and up the Nevada road to Fort Independence. The gist of them was this: if the law can't catch this bastard, Orozco, send the army.

The pressure had been building for months, and on the second of June, Company I, 1st Cavalry had ridden into the fort after a long march from Reno, Nevada. Now they met with the influential Barker's representatives, and the troopers soon had their orders. They were to search out all bandits, Orozco in particular.

They reached Sierra Gorda, and their commanding officer met with Barker. The commander was Captain Virgil Truett, and he was the veteran of several skirmishes against the Walker Lake Paiutes. "Heard about Orozco taking the woman," he said. "I also heard he saved her from renegade Indians."

"What difference does that make?"

The captain shrugged. "None really, I suppose. Except it may prove he isn't all bad."

"Captain, he killed two miners down on the Yellow Grade Road recently. Shot them down in cold blood after robbing them. One of them lived long enough to tell us he bragged he was Orozco. The one who told us that was one of my best foremen. Don't waste any sympathy on him."

"That being the case," the cavalry officer said, "I won't. He ought to be shot down like a dog."

Orozco was in bad shape. Belle kept looking at him. She was still lashed to her horse, but her hands were free. He suddenly started to topple and she reined over quickly and held out her hand to stop him. Nuñez turned to look back and saw what was happening.

"He's got to have rest."

"Too bad. Is no rest. Not with them two hombres back there." He grinned at her. "But maybe we stop for ambush, eh? We kill that gringo hombre of yours."

"No!"

"You right. Sabás, he in no condition for

fight now. I know a place for to rest."

"It got to be soon, Lázaro," Orozco said.

"It going to be soon, Sabás."

"Where?"

"Near the place called by the gringos Post Office Springs. But I know a place in back, they don't find. I hide there many times."

"There is many bad gringos visit those springs," Orozco said. "Some, they bad as you and me."

"So? You afraid they going to rob us?" Nuñez laughed at his own joke.

"You can't trust no gringo bandidos," Orozco said. "You know that. They don't got honesty."

"You right, amigo. Well, we watch out for them unhonest bandidos, eh?"

"Mostly I worry about the woman."

"I see that nobody touch her, Sabás. Only you and me."

"I don't like that too."

"You hard for to please anymore," Nuñez said. He rode up ahead, as if he had no fear of whether Orozco was pleased or not.

Orozco said in a low voice, "I'm sorry, Belle. But maybe I don't going to make it. And if I kill Lázaro, and I die, you be alone in the desert. Then you die."

"You're forgetting the man riding behind us."

Orozco straightened in his saddle. "No, I don't forget that. Well, you belong to me now, long as I live."

"Please. If you love me, you'll kill that fat pig friend of yours and let my man find me."

"He no is your man now. I am."

"If you love me —"

"Do I ever say I *love* you, Belle? I only say I *want* you."

For a moment she was angered by his reply. Then ruefully she admitted to herself that his feeling was no different from what she had for him. There was a madness between them that had little to do with love.

Post Office Springs had a reason for its name.

The law in the region, as John Leslie had seen in Sierra Gorda, was loosely organized. This held true in other camps as far away as Lida, Austin, White Pine, and Pioche. In these places, for want of constituted authority, punishment for crime was sometimes simple banishment.

From Sierra Gorda a hardcase offender would occasionally be shown the High Sierras forty miles to the west and the sand-fringed Panamint Mountains forty miles to the east, and told to make a choice but to get the hell out of town or be hanged.

171

The Sierras offered bitterly harsh winters and few pickings for those of criminal tendencies. The Panamints offered a modicum of wood, water, and some game. So the Panamints had become a refuge of sorts for the desert banditti, as well as for an occasional escapee from the Nevada State Prison at Carson City to the north.

The Springs itself had become a crossroads turnoff for the sanctuary. Here a small source of water was half-hidden under some thorny mesquite.

And here, too, in certain spots among the adjacent rocks were left, from time to time, messages between members of the owlhoot fraternity.

"The name is odd," Belle said.

"Lázaro's?"

"Post Office Springs."

Orozco smiled wanly. "Is a gringo joke, I think. But sometimes they leave letters."

"Will we stop there?"

"For water, sure. For letters, no."

"Are there never any for you?"

"For a Mexican? I don't read *inglés*. And Lázaro, he don't read nothing." His smile left him. "Them gringo bandidos, they don't want no Mexicans messing around them messages, anyhow."

"How do you know that?"

"I only make joke, Belle. But I think is maybe so."

"If I could leave a message for Johnny —"

"Johnny?"

"That man of mine who follows."

"Hah! And what you going to tell your Johnny?"

"I'll ask him not to kill you. I'll ask him not to track you down."

"You think he listen to what you ask?"

"He might. I will tell him you saved me from the Paiutes."

He looked thoughtfully at her. "I think, Belle, you don't worried about me. You worried about this Johnny."

"I'm worried about you both. Don't you understand? I care for you both."

Nuñez had been listening and now he said, "And for Lázaro, gringa. Don't you forget how much you care for me." He laughed.

Orozco said, "Your hombre, how he going to know is messages in this place? Don't you told me he just come from Arizona?"

"I could put it in plain sight," Belle said.

His words about Arizona chilled her with thought of Benteen, who was really Sutter, seeking revenge against Johnny for the death of his brother. She had recognized the man whom they had rushed back in the canyon. She had got a good glimpse of him through

173

the dust and the gun smoke, and she could no longer tell herself she was mistaken. She was certain now it was Benteen. Sutter, really.

It was the man she had set out for Sierra Gorda to warn Johnny about. The man she was sure would still be out for vengeance.

She could not imagine why he was teamed now with Johnny, but she knew that whatever the reason the danger was still there. If only she could warn Johnny of this too.

She said, "Please, Sabás. When we stop at the spring, let me leave a message."

"Sure, Belle, if you want. But what you write on? We don't got no paper. We don't got no pencil neither."

She had no answer for that.

But Nuñez did. He reached into a pocket and pulled out a small black book. "Is some pages that don't got print," he said. He rode close to Belle and handed it to her. "You tell your man to don't follow us no more."

She looked at the book and was shocked. "This is a Bible — a New Testament!"

Nuñez grinned. "Bible? I don't know that. Big joke, eh?"

"Where did you get it?"

"I rob it from one those miners I kill."

"You didn't!" She was aghast.

"Chure. Why no? I been religious. Onetime altar boy."

"You still don't got a pencil," Orozco said.

Nuñez fished in another pocket. "Here is." He held a pencil out to Belle.

She was afraid to ask, but Orozco said, "And where you get that, Lázaro?"

"From the other miner I kill. What you think?"

CHAPTER 11

A week before, during the evening lockup routine in the Nevada State Prison at Carson City, twelve convicts had overpowered the guards, smashed their way into the arsenal, and armed themselves. In the ensuing action they freed seventeen other inmates, killed three officials, and took off down the California-Nevada border. Most of them were soon caught and sent back to the prison. Some were killed by the pursuing guards. Six escaped.

A week after the breakout, these six had reached Post Office Springs, which had been previously known to two of them before their incarceration.

These two, after relieving their thirst, immediately rummaged around in the rocks for messages that might guide their immediate future. Mostly they were looking for news of possible acquaintances and the activities of the latter.

Big Dave Brown was the leader. He was the one who had hatched the escape plan, and none of his companions questioned his assumed command.

What he found most interesting among the messages was the one that Belle had written a few hours before:

To John Leslie, from Belle Jackson:
John, Please do not try to kill Orozco. He treats me well, and I am grateful that he saved me from vicious Paiutes. I do not want either of you killed. I will somehow survive.
P.S. Beware of partners you may pick up, please, please, please!

Belle

There wasn't much more she could have written on the torn-out flyleaf of a pocket-size New Testament.

Big Dave was intrigued by the note.

There were a couple of reasons for this. One, he knew Orozco, as he had known Vásquez, from an earlier time. He was aware that there was a price on Orozco's head. And, two, he at once thought of a possible means of securing amnesty where he and his cohorts could live perhaps comfortably during the long hot months of summer. Sierra Gorda was the biggest and the best of the area mining towns. And the law there, he had heard, was tolerant of anything short of murder.

Big Dave was an imaginative man, and he

had his newest plan worked out in a matter of minutes. Quickly he explained it to his former cell mate, Charlie Dodge, who also knew Orozco.

Dodge had long ago decided that Big Dave was a cut above most outlaws when it came to thinking. He readily agreed with Big Dave's plan, and they soon convinced the others.

"We bring Orozco in to Sierra Gorda and we'll be heroes," Big Dave said. "After all, ain't none of us wanted in California. We got a number of talents amongst us that we can use in a town like that. It could mean living high on the hog for a change, boys. What do you say? Plenty of food, likker, and easy women."

He had a chorus of agreeing voices.

"How we going to find him?" Dodge said.

"Hell, this note is brand-new written," Brown said. "Him and this Belle woman can't be more than a day away."

"Let's get to tracking," one of the others said. "I'm hungry, thirsty for likker, and lustful."

They were in Nuñez's hideout, which wasn't much to Belle's way of thinking. A mere overhanging of cliff screened by high greasewood and mesquite.

"I don't think we safe here," Orozco said.

"I don't ask what you think," Nuñez said.

"You got to rest some. So we stop here. You sleep, amigo. Pretty soon we move on." He paused, seeing doubt in Orozco's tired face. "I don't going to bother your *mujer* none."

"You promise?"

"By my mother's milk," Lázaro said.

Orozco sighed and lay down, easing his position to lessen the pain of his wounded shoulder. He either passed out or fell asleep immediately.

Nuñez moved several yards away and sat down. He motioned Belle to him.

She went toward him reluctantly, and halted several steps away.

"We got to talk," he said. "You don't want bother Sabás sleep, eh?"

She came closer after a moment. "What do you want?"

He pulled out his six-gun. "I tell you something, Belle. You make *grito,* you make cry, and I kill Sabás with one shot."

"Why would I cry?"

"I don't know. You smart, you don't." He reached out then with his free hand and grabbed her leg and jerked, and she fell beside him. "Now, you and me, we have some fun. I get tired of waiting." He grabbed her into his arms like some great smelly bear, and he crushed her mouth painfully with his own.

179

She tried to struggle, but she was held as if in a vise.

He drew his mouth away and said, "You want I kill Sabás? You and me. Now! You understand?"

She saw the cruelty in his eyes and knew he meant what he said. She wavered for only a moment, then went limp.

He reached down a big hand and lifted her skirt high, then ripped away at her undergarments. She began to cry and this seemed only to fuel his lust.

A moment later he was mounting her.

Big Dave Brown said, "Christ!" and shot Lázaro Nuñez through the head.

The rest of the escaped convicts stared with mixed expressions at the scene. Charlie Dodge was scowling. The one who had said he was lustful licked his lips and did not take his eyes off Belle lying there exposed from the waist down.

Orozco had jerked up at the sound of the shot and grabbed for his gun lying beside him.

Big Dave had already swung his weapon. "Hold it, Sabás!"

Sabás held it, surprised at the calling of his name. "Brown!" he said. "Why you point that gun at Orozco?"

"Sorry, amigo, but I got a reason."

"You goddamn gringos, you always got a reason."

"We're reasonable people," Brown said. "That's why you *cholos* don't appreciate us."

Orozco was no longer looking at him. He was staring at Belle, who was pulling down her clothes to cover herself. And at Lázaro lying beside her with half his head blown away.

"Well, you done one good thing, gringo," he said to Brown. "You got my thanks for that. She is *my* woman."

"My pleasure," Big Dave said. "But I give you the chance to pay back the favor. All you got to do is come along peaceable to Sierra Gorda."

"What for?"

"Like I said, amigo. I got a reason."

"I don't."

"I'll give you one," Brown said. "Your woman there. You come along without trouble and I won't let nothing happen to her. You give us trouble, and I'll turn these hombres of mine loose on her."

Orozco did not answer.

Big Dave jerked his head at the one who was still staring at Belle. "Jason there, he's been locked up for six years. If I let him loose, no telling what he might do to her. He was doing time for beating his own woman to death."

"I guess I don't got no choice," Orozco said.

"That's what I like, a reasonable *cholo*."

"You goddamn gringos, you all alike."

Big Dave grinned. "No," he said, "we only *look* alike to you greasers."

Jason said, "Ain't we going to have some fun with the girl?"

"No," Big Dave said.

"Why the hell not?"

"Because I said so," Big Dave said. "Mount up. We got some horses now. If there ain't enough to go around, we'll take turns riding."

"You sure they're going to welcome us at Sierra Gorda?" Charlie Dodge said.

"I ain't sure. But I'm guessing. And if they give us trouble instead, we got six men with guns. We can shoot our way out again. Hell, they're mostly only miners."

"I don't see how you can waste that woman," Jason said.

"I don't figure to," Big Dave said. But he didn't explain what he meant by that.

It was near evening of the next day when the convict bunch rode up to Sierra Gorda, flanking Orozco and Belle who were tied to their horses.

Barker himself appeared within minutes

after their arrival. "I'm Amos Barker."

"Name of Brown, Mr. Barker. Dave Brown. Me and my friends here brought you a present."

Barker stared at Orozco without expression. Orozco stared back.

Without turning his head, Barker said, "Who is the woman?"

"Name of Belle Jackson, I understand."

"Untie her, you damn fool. She was taken by Orozco."

"Is that a fact? Then how come she's so worried about his wound?"

"Untie her."

Big Dave said, "Jason! Do what the man says."

"Sure." Jason dismounted and went over to Belle and began fumbling with her ankle bonds. He alternately stroked and pinched her as he worked.

She cringed under his touch. Freed, she got out of the saddle quickly and moved over to stand near Barker.

Barker faced her. "I am glad to see you free, ma'am." He eyed her appreciatively.

She noted that and wondered if she could use his appreciation to help Sabás. She said, "Orozco is wounded."

"He is a bandit, ma'am."

"He saved me from marauding Indians."

"Yes, I heard. And how did he treat you afterward?" There was a real curiosity in his tone.

"As a gentleman. Without him I would have died."

"Out of character for his kind, I'd say."

"You doubt me?"

"I never doubt the word of a lady."

"Will you get a doctor for him?"

"What for? We're going to give him a miners' court trial, then hang him. It would be a waste to patch him up first."

Big Dave spoke up. "How about us, Mr. Barker? We brought him in. Ain't there a reward out on him?"

"We ought to hang all of you with him. We had word here of a breakout up at Carson City. You're wearing clothes that look suspicious."

"Forget the reward," Brown said. "But we got guns in the hands of men who know how to use them. You'd play hell trying to take us with these pick and shovelers you got in camp here." He paused. "All we want is a place to live."

Amos Barker looked again at Orozco, the Mexican who had smashed his heirloom watch. Orozco, delivered now into his hands for suitable punishment by hanging. I am not an ungrateful man, he thought.

He said, "On two conditions. One, you don't in any way impede the working of the mines. Two, you don't commit any crimes here. You agree, you can stay. But if you violate these conditions, I'll come after you with every man in my hire. We'll beat you to death with those shovels."

Big Dave gave him an easy smile. "It's agreed then. And you got yourself a Mex bandit to hang for entertainment."

"I'm going to enjoy that," Barker said. "Did you know he stole my watch?"

"What?"

"My favorite watch. The son of a bitch greaser stole my watch."

Big Dave exchanged glances with Orozco. He said, "Christ! I'm glad I ain't a Mexican."

Orozco was in the small jail built of mining timbers. It had a high iron-barred window opening and a similar, smaller opening in a heavy sheet metal door.

It was early morning and, although it was July, it was not yet stuffy in the jail. The seven-thousand-foot altitude gave Sierra Gorda a late-night chill.

Forty-odd miles to the east, the floor of Death Valley would be already turning into the furnace it daily became, he thought. But he would have gladly exchanged places. He would have been safe there. Nobody, not even a bunch of traitorous gringo outlaws, would have bothered him there. Not in the summer.

Fatalistically, now he accepted his plight. He could see no way out. He was caught and he would hang. Ironically, the soreness had mostly left his wounded shoulder, and much of his natural strength had returned. I am going to feel *bien* when they hang me, he thought grimly. Goddamn!

From outside the noises that accompanied mining activities drifted in. The mountain at Sierra Gorda was an anthill of activity, he thought. Them goddamn gringos, they don't never rest.

If he stood on his toes and clung to the bars of the window and craned his neck, he was able to see the top few hundred feet of the giant aerial tramway, steam-driven, which carried the big ore buckets down to Barker's smelter three thousand feet below.

It was a fascinating thing to watch as the big buckets, filled with silver ore, swung off into space. At times during the descent, when those buckets were crossing low spots in the mountainside, they would be a couple of hundred feet in the air.

Orozco watched until his interest waned, then lay on the bare plank bunk and stared at the flat, timbered roof. He could still hear the clank and the squeal and the growl of the operating tram. Them goddamn buckets, he thought, they fly off into the sky like big birds. I wish one of them was me.

He hoped Belle was all right. That big, important gringo, Barker, who hated him, he was taking an interest in her maybe. Well, he, Sabás, had had her for a while. It was the one good thing he could look back on in recent months. He had felt the end was closing in on him, but he was surprised it had come so suddenly. One day I have Belle in my arms and I am happy, he mused. Next day, goddamn, I am wish I am a ore bucket. So I could fly.

He heard her voice at the door. He was sure of it. Even through the clatter of the mining machinery, he knew it was her.

He was at the door in an instant, trying to peek through the tiny open squares between the wide crossed-iron straps.

"Belle! You come to see Sabás."

"I would have come sooner. But I couldn't get away from that big boss, Barker."

"He treat you all right?"

"He got me a room in the hotel."

"What you tell him?"

"What do you mean?" Belle said.

"What you think I mean?"

"I told him I have to go back to Los Angeles."

"You going to wait till they hang Orozco?"

"Please! Oh, Sabás, how can I help?"

He shrugged, though she could not see him in the dimness behind the bars. "I don't think you can, Belle. I just stay here a little while and dream I wish I am a ore bucket."

"What?"

"I keep watch them ore bucket swing out in the sky like a bird, and I wish I am."

There was a silence, then she gasped. "Sabás! The tram!"

"*Sí*, Belle. The tram."

"If you could — But how —"

"What you mean, Belle?"

"If you could get out of this jail —"

"There don't be no way."

"I can't let them hang you!"

"You a nice lady, Belle. Now I tell you I love you. But you don't can help Sabás now. More better you go away and forget."

"No!"

"What you can do?"

"I'm going to talk to Barker."

"He don't let me go. I rob his goddamn watch, and he don't never forget."

"I'm going to talk to him."

"It take more than talk, Belle."

She was silent. Then she said, "If it does, so be it."

188

He strained to see her face, but she was gone.

"He didn't kill those two miners near here a few days ago," Belle said.

"You say that," Amos Barker said. They were sitting in the lobby of the American Hotel.

"Lázaro Nuñez did it. I heard him admit to the killings himself. He put the blame on Orozco. His idea of a joke, as I said."

"Maybe. But even so, Orozco has other killings to his credit."

"How many are laid to him mistakenly?"

Barker shrugged. "Some, possibly. But he's done his share, no doubt."

"You are set on hanging him?"

"What would you do to stop me?" His eyes kept roving over her. John Leslie's woman, he thought. The risk of it titillated him, even as a risky business venture sometimes did. John Leslie, the gunfighter's woman.

"What would it take?"

"Suppose I said if you slept with me it would help?" His eyes were on her face now, a faint smile playing on his wide, hard mouth. "Would you go that far to help that greaser?"

"Would you stop the hanging?"

He seemed to get a satisfaction out of her

answer. "You would degrade yourself for him?"

"Would you stop the hanging?"

The pleasure on his face was almost ecstatic. "No," he said.

She had been tense. Suddenly she felt weak and listless. "You had to make me say it, didn't you?"

"I get my kicks in strange ways," he said. "Besides the son of a bitch took my watch."

"I will go now, Mr. Barker. To my room."

"You will hear some commotion when we take him up to the tram derrick to hang him," Barker said. "If you want to witness his trial immediately before that, it will be held at two o'clock. In the Miners Hall. We will hang him promptly at three."

The trial was as she had known it would be.

Barker sat to one side, up front facing an audience of white, off-shift miners. A miner named Pat Fraley sat on a raised platform with a small table in front of him to serve as the judge's bench.

The prosecutor was a Wells Fargo agent whose stages had been periodically hit by various robbers, including, he had already stated to the court, the defendant, one Sabás Orozco, now seated before them.

There was no defense counsel.

The prosecuting agent interrogated the defendant.

"Are you Sabás Orozco?"

"You know it."

"Do you deny robbing stages, freight wagons, stage and freight agents, travelers, and other innocent victims during your lengthy career of crime."

"Sure, I deny it."

"You're a goddamn liar."

Barker broke in loudly. "Ask him about my watch. Make him say he stepped on it."

The prosecutor said, "What did you do with Mr. Barker's watch."

"I smash it with my boot."

"Mean Mexican bastard, aren't you?"

"Gringos treat me bad sometimes. I get mad."

"Besides that you killed two miners last week on the Yellow Grade Road."

Belle stood up in the audience. "He didn't do that. A bandit named Lázaro Nuñez did it. I heard Nuñez say so."

"Aren't you the woman that Orozco here abducted?"

She hesitated. "He rescued me from some drunken Paiutes."

"And you've been living with him ever since."

There was some amused muttering among the spectators, and a guffaw here and there. Belle was silent.

Pat Fraley, the judge, had a leer on his face. He said, "Answer the question."

"Of course I've been living with him, you damn fools," Belle said. "How could I get away?"

"You had your say," Fraley said. "Sit down!"

Belle sat, knowing the futility of it all.

"This court sentences the accused to hang by his goddamned neck until he's dead. Sentence to be carried out immediately!" Fraley said.

Belle met Orozco's eyes. He showed no emotion. Then he smiled faintly and formed a kiss with his lips for her.

Tears blurred her vision as the miners crowded around to hustle him from the hall.

They began the short climb up toward the top tram trestle. She mingled in the crowd that followed.

CHAPTER 12

Orozco stood stoically as a rope was thrown over a timber of the trestle, and as Barker himself slid the noose wide, preparing to drop it over his head.

Orozco's hands were not bound. They were left free so that those watching could witness his desperate clutch later as he slowly strangled. He wouldn't be dropped, he would be hoisted. It made a better show that way.

Belle forced her way over to where she had been earlier that day after her discussion with Barker. From behind a leg of the trestle she reached down and withdrew a carbine.

She was at this time only five yards away from Barker.

The tram had been stopped for the hanging, and a few feet away was one of the empty ore buckets, waiting to be loaded.

"Stop right now!" she called to Barker. She held the gun pointed at his big belly. "Get in the bucket," she said to Orozco.

He moved fast to leap inside it. She handed him the carbine. "Keep it on Barker," she said, and got in beside him. "Start up the tram," she said to the mine owner.

Barker seemed amused by it all. "There's no steam up," he said.

"There's enough," she said. "It was running not ten minutes ago. Start it or Sabás will blow you to hell."

Barker stepped over to the control lever and started it up. There were guns in the crowd, but Orozco still held his pointed at Barker, and nobody moved. They, like Barker, seemed not too perturbed by the turn of events. It bothered Belle that they appeared entertained. Something must be wrong.

She and Sabás swung off into the air, the bucket swinging violently. Orozco fought to hold his balance and his aim as he kept the carbine barrel poked over the top of the bucket.

They were two hundred yards out and a hundred feet above the sloping terrain when Barker halted the tram.

"Get down!" Orozco said. He pulled her down until they were lying together in the bottom of the bucket.

Bullets began to smack against its iron side.

Belle flinched. "We're no better off," she said. "Worse, maybe."

"Maybe for you," he said. "But for me is better. You save my life, Belle."

"They will haul us back up again," she said.

Orozco thought for a moment, then shook

his head. "I don't think is so. This tram, I think, it only go one direction. One side, it go up. The other side, this one, it go down."

"Then they could leave us here to die!"

"No, they don't do that. They got to use the tram for ore."

Another barrage slammed against the bucket.

"Why do they do that?" she cried.

He grinned. "They having fun, Belle. Them goddamn gringos, they like shoot at a Mexican — and his woman." He put his arm around her. "How you like make love here, Belle?"

She shoved away from him. "Are you crazy?"

He laughed, then said seriously, "Pretty soon they get tired fooling around. They start us moving again then."

Almost at once it happened. The cable tautened, and with a jerk they began to descend.

"They got hombres down there now," he said. "They waiting for us."

John Leslie and Benteen had picked out the trail again. Or rather Benteen had. It took some time, but eventually he had read the story.

"Six men came from the north," he said. "They tracked the two Mexes and Belle back

195

into that overhang. They killed that big, fat one there and took Orozco and her with them, heading north again."

"A posse?"

"Can't you read sign at all? They were walking when they got here."

There was no need to track now. They simply followed the dusty stage road. Benteen kept his eye on the road skirt for signs of riders leaving it, but there was none.

"Let's see that map," Leslie said.

Benteen fished it out of his pocket and handed it over.

Leslie studied it as they rode, then said, "They could be heading for Sierra Gorda."

"My guess too."

"Right back where I started from."

"Happens that way sometimes."

"Damn good thing I stumbled onto you," Leslie said. "For me, I mean. I'd have lost them a long time ago."

Benteen stared straight ahead without answering. The expression on his weathered face was set. He kept clenching and unclenching his jaw as if with effort to hold back a retort.

Leslie noted this and wondered at it. Benteen was cold as ice, he thought. But he did not strike Leslie as being a hard case. He was a hard one to figure. It was as though he bore a resentment toward Leslie for having been the one to rescue him from the mine shaft. It all seemed mighty strange, Leslie thought. He wondered if he'd ever know the why of the man's behavior.

They stopped that night at the mining town of Darwin, which they judged to be halfway to Sierra Gorda. Darwin was now two years past its peak, but in its boom days it had had two smelters, twenty operating mines, and seven hundred citizens. It had fed its share of silver into the coffers of Los Angeles, as had many other strikes among these barren hills and mountains.

But none had ever compared to the richness of Sierra Gorda.

It was midafternoon as they reached the foot of the big mountain. Leslie reined up and stared.

"The tram must be broke down," he said. "It's stopped."

"Ever do that before?" Benteen said.

"Once in a while. When it does, they fall back on the standby ore wagons to haul the stuff down."

They rode closer, and suddenly the tram was moving again.

Benteen grunted but kept on without stopping to look. "We better be thinking about that bunch that took the Mex and Belle."

"I've been thinking."

"And what did you come up with?"

Leslie shrugged. "Nothing yet. We don't even know who's got her."

"She's your woman, not mine."

Leslie held back a comment and swung his eyes upward at the descending buckets heaped with silver ore. "Christ!" he said. "Look at that!"

Benteen looked up.

"People!" Leslie said. "One of those buckets has got people in it!"

"Hell of a way to go for a ride," Benteen said.

"It can't be for fun."

"Couple of drunks maybe."

They watched as the buckets descended.

"One is a woman," Leslie said.

"I told you. A drunk whore and her customer out for a fun ride."

"One is a Mex, I think."

Benteen studied the approaching couple.

"Let's get over to that tram shed," Leslie said.

"You think —"

"I do."

"Interesting lady friend you got," Benteen said. "That Belle, she's some kind of woman. What the hell next will she get into?"

Leslie didn't answer. He was too intent on

finding out what was waiting for her in that tram shed. He said, "If they know about Belle and that shooting at Lone Willow —"

"My thought exactly," Benteen said. "They'll lynch Orozco for sure. And they just might get carried away and make it a double ceremony."

"I've seen lynch mobs before."

"Yeah. Me too." Benteen paused. "There's another thing. If they hang Orozco, I'm going to lose out on that reward."

"I'm interested in Belle."

"Yeah. I'd hate to see a woman like that with her neck stretched."

They were close now to the crude building that housed the tram machinery at the bottom end. A Wells Fargo stage stood waiting by it, empty except for the driver waiting beside it.

They rode up and Leslie said, "What's going on here?" He gestured at the tram bucket nearing the bottom.

The man near the stage said, "That bucket's got Orozco and a woman that helped him escape a hanging up above. Reckon they'll hang the both of them now."

"Who will?"

"Got half a dozen men inside the shed there. I brung them down because the stage was handy. Told me to wait. Reckon they'll want to ride back up to finish what they started."

"The woman is innocent."

"How do you know that?" the driver said. "Anyhow, she ain't now. Not after she held a gun on Mr. Barker to get that bastard loose. Besides, there's a rumor she shot some kid at a stage station." He stopped and looked closely at Leslie. "Hell, ain't you John Leslie, the marshal here in Sierra Gorda? You ought to know about this."

"Just rode in," Leslie said quickly. "Keep an eye on our horses. I'm going in there."

"Sure. But you ain't going to stop that hanging, Marshal."

"Didn't say I was," Leslie said, dismounting.

Benteen swung down too, and they moved fast toward the machinery structure, each reaching to loosen his revolver in its holster.

Five miners and Barker were inside, waiting.

Barker gave Leslie and Benteen a close look each. He said to Leslie, "Well, Marshal, you've been wasting your time looking for Orozco. We've got him and your girl about to drop into our hands."

"Good!"

"Not so good for you, maybe, when you know the truth of it," Barker said. He seemed to be enjoying this. "It seems she's got a strong case on that Mexican bastard. She saved him from a hanging up above. Surprised us. She won't again."

The descending bucket was getting near.

What Barker had said was what Leslie had been fearing might be true. It hit him hard in the gut, and he said nothing.

The five miners crowded around the cable winch, stared at Leslie, then switched their glances back to the tramway as they waited. There was anticipation in their faces. The bloodlust was there.

Leslie whipped out his gun and shoved it into Barker's ribs.

Benteen covered the miners.

"I'm taking Belle out of here," Leslie said.

"Go ahead," Barker said. "Be a fool. But leave Orozco."

The bucket reached bottom and Orozco leaped out. He stood, startled at the sight of the drawn guns holding Barker and his men. He had left the carbine in the ore container.

Leslie said, "Get out of the bucket, Belle."

"Johnny! You!" She climbed out and stood still, her emotions holding her from further movement. Her eyes were on Leslie's face, and something akin to shame showed on her own.

Leslie said to her, "Go out and get on my roan."

She did not move immediately. She wanted to warn him that Benteen was really Sutter. She said, "Your partner, there, he's —"

"Go!" he said roughly. "I'll join you in a minute."

She still hesitated, looking now at Orozco.

Orozco said, "Do it, Belle, what he says." He gave a slight nod.

She turned and went out.

"You got your woman," Barker said. "Now get the hell out of my sight."

Orozco saw their guns still held. He looked at Leslie and at Benteen, then held on Benteen's stare. Benteen jerked his head, almost imperceptibly, in Belle's direction. Orozco slipped out of the shed.

"Stop him, you fool!" Barker said. "That's Orozco!"

Benteen made a show of rushing out, gun in hand.

Leslie was surprised by Benteen's action. He removed his gun from Barker's ribs. What the hell was Benteen doing?

Barker turned on him. "You've let him get away."

Benteen's gun blasted outside.

"Wasn't *my* intention," Leslie said. "Belle's the one I wanted." He made for the door.

More gunfire sounded. This time from a carbine. He remembered the saddle guns on

202

the horses. He got out in time to see Orozco and Belle riding away together.

Benteen said, "They got away."

"Why Belle?"

"I heard him holler they'd hang her too for helping him. She spooked, I reckon."

"You could have stopped her."

"I didn't think she'd join him," Benteen said. He sounded as if he believed it.

"I ought to hang the both of you," Barker said, "for interfering."

"It was Belle I was looking out for," Leslie said.

"Sure," Benteen said smoothly. "Both of us."

"You damn bunglers."

"We'll get on his trail again, Mr. Barker," Benteen said. He turned to the stage driver. "Get up on the box. We'll chase them with the coach."

"Are you crazy?"

"Get on the box," Benteen said. "I've killed men with this gun."

The driver said, "Mr. Barker?"

Barker's face was furious, but he said, "Go ahead. The story doesn't sound right, but go ahead."

Leslie got on the seat beside the driver, and Benteen climbed up on top. The driver started the team and took off along the road south at a run. They could see the dust kicked up by Orozco and Belle a couple of miles ahead.

Leslie said to Benteen, "What the hell did you pull off back there?"

Benteen said, "I'm not letting anybody beat me out of that reward."

Leslie said to the stage driver, "You know something about this country. Where do you think he'll go?"

The driver was a long time answering. Finally he said, "Was I him, with men closing in on me, I'd take the trail east out of Darwin and hightail it through the Panamints and into Death Valley."

"Hot this time of year, ain't it?"

"Hotter than the hubs of hell. And that'd be the reason I'd go there. Ain't no posse, or bounty hunter neither, going in there in the summer, not even for Orozco."

"That bad?"

"Hell, Marshal, the temperature there gets up to a hundred and thirty or better during the day. No water. I went through there once in the winter. Most desolate goddamn country on earth. In the summer — well, I reckon in the summer is when it got its name. There's a lot more dead men there than ever got through it alive this time of year."

"Wouldn't Orozco know all that?"

"I reckon he's been there before. If anybody could survive there, it'd be him. The son of a bitch has got to know the desert better than anybody. Christ, when he comes out of the brush to rob a stage, he's always shaved clean like he was one of them theayter actors that plays the mining towns sometimes."

"Try to keep his dust in sight," Leslie said. "We'll get horses at Darwin."

"You going into Death Valley after him if he goes? Hell, you'll be a greenhorn over there."

"Maybe."

They kept up the pace, not speaking. Then the driver said, "She must be one hell of a woman."

"Yeah," John Leslie said.

She was a hell of a woman all right, he thought. He didn't like the idea of why she had saved Orozco, but he had to admire her courage in doing it. He could not let himself brood about her reason. It would drive him mad with jealousy.

It was evening when the driver pulled up in front of the Darwin Livery. "You need mounts, saddles, a pack animal," he said. "This is the place to get them." He paused. "That Mex bandit and the girl took off with your rifles too. Well, you can get near anything in this town, if you got the money."

And that could be a problem, Leslie thought. He said, "Thanks for your help."

The man looked at him. "Hell, there wasn't much else I could do, was there?"

"Yeah, you're right."

"And Barker ordered me to do it. I'll let the stage company argue with him." He hesitated, then said, "I wish you luck, Marshal, getting back your woman. Too bad that Orozco got away from your partner."

Benteen caught the driver's eye and said, "You figure I did it intentional?"

"No, sir!" the driver said. "I surely do not!"

"All right then," Benteen said.

"Adiós," the driver said. He got the team moving and drove off toward the Darwin stage station.

Leslie frowned. "Maybe he don't. But I do."

"I come a long way after that reward money," Benteen said. "Like I told you, I wasn't going to let that rich bastard of a mine owner cut me out of it."

"Did you think about Belle?"

"Not right then."

"Mercenary bastard, ain't you? Cold-blooded."

Benteen's face took on that look that Leslie had seen before. "Not as cold-blooded as some I know," Benteen said.

Between the two of them they pooled enough money for a couple of fair horses, worn saddles, but no pack animal.

"What do you know about Death Valley?" Leslie asked the livery man.

"I know enough to stay out this time of year."

Benteen said, "You see a Mexican and a white woman ride through here earlier?"

"Nope. They heading into that valley in July, they won't come out. They'll die."

They paid the hostler and rode over to a hardware store to spend most of what they had left on a pair of carbines, cartridges, and canteens, and then went to a grocery store where they spent the rest on bacon, flour, coffee, and a few canned goods.

"We better get that Mex bastard," Benteen said. "I didn't figure my expenses would come this high."

"You chasing a Mexican?" the storekeeper said. "Riding with a woman?"

"You see them?"

"Went through an hour or two ago while I was sitting on the porch there. Took that road that winds northeast into the Panamint range. I paid some notice on account they was a mismatched pair, her being white it appeared." He paused. "I took notice, too, because ain't nobody goes that way in the hot months."

"That's the road into Death Valley?"

"Yep. Forty miles of rough go and you'll reach Emigrant Junction where them Jayhawkers lost their way. From there on you'll descend into hell." The storekeeper paused. "You chasing them?" he said again.

"Maybe."

"Well, you better catch up to them before they get there, or you'll all end up dead."

"I got to get that woman away from him," Leslie said. "She's mine."

"She didn't look like she was unwilling, the way they rode."

"I'm telling you how it is," Leslie said.

"Hell, mister, I didn't mean no offense."

CHAPTER 13

"We lost some time back there," Leslie said.

"Don't matter much. Way that storekeeper told it, there's only one way in from this direction." Benteen paused. "Didn't say about getting out."

"He said something. Said we might not get out."

"Something to think about, ain't it?"

"You don't sound worried."

"I can beat any goddamn desert," Benteen said. "I know all the Apache tricks."

"This won't be Apache country."

"No. I heard someplace there's a handful of Shoshone live there though. If they stand it, I can." Benteen gave him a studied look.

"I wasn't thinking about us," Leslie said. "I was thinking about Belle."

Benteen rode in silence for a time, then said, "Too bad she got herself mixed up with that son of a bitch."

"Wasn't her doing. Not in the beginning anyway." Leslie hesitated, thinking back to something Belle had tried to tell him during the action at the tram. Something about "your partner —" He looked at Benteen, wondering about it now when it was too late. He said, "I never did understand what she was doing on that stage to Sierra Gorda. The time when Orozco took her. She must have had a good reason."

Benteen met his stare. "Yeah. You have any idea what it was?"

"None at all."

"Hard to figure a woman," Benteen said.

They crossed the Panamint Valley and began to climb into the Panamints. Ahead, the range rose a mile high or better. Far toward the south a peak rose sentinel-like to twice that height. There was timber on those higher reaches, but the slopes below were barren.

It was a somber land, dun and gray. Sagebrush and greasewood had claimed most of it, the range as well as the lowlands. And over the range, through the high pass ahead, what could they expect?

The sun was going down and they made dry camp just off the trail, thankful they had watered the horses miles back at Panamint Springs. Dark fell and a moon showed, and the dull, bleak land was transformed, as if the silver it hid had surfaced.

It made Leslie think again of Belle over there somewhere alone with Orozco. He could not sleep and cast off his blanket from time to time, jealousy and rage roiling in him.

Benteen looked over at him, guessed his turmoil, and took satisfaction from it. Then his own rage took over as he thought of how his kid brother had died by Leslie's gun.

Once we get Orozco, he thought. Once I got the Mex on a saddle, dead or alive. Then you'll get yours, my fast-gun marshal friend. He savored the taste of vengeance coming.

Until he remembered himself trapped in the bottom of that mine shaft and about to die. "You goddamn bastard!" he said then silently to John Leslie, and began to call him a string of other names.

They went up the long ascent toward the pass that led to the valley. The trail reached up to where a cover of piñon and juniper began.

Benteen gestured. "Any Injuns around, they'd find food here. Piñon nuts."

"Reckon we'll meet any?"

Benteen shrugged. "What I hear, they'll be mighty poor. Digger Injuns, they're called. Poorest breed of Shoshone. Those few we seen in Darwin was Paiutes, which is a close cousin. Whites call them Diggers too, account of they use sharp sticks to dig for roots and bugs to eat. Country like this, they'll eat anything they can swallow."

"How the hell could they live down in

Death Valley this time of year?"

"Don't reckon they could. Was why I thought about the piñon nuts and such. They'd come up here when the heat gets too bad to stand." Benteen looked above them. "Be some game up there, at least small. Maybe even a few bighorn sheep."

"I didn't know there was Shoshones this far west," Leslie said.

"Big nation. They spread all over the western plateau from the Rockies to the Sierras and beyond, I reckon. These out here, the western Shoshones, they got to be the poorest of the lot."

"Warriors?"

"Nothing like those in the Rockies. But fifteen, twenty years back, they raised some hell up Walker Lake, Nevada way. Those were the Paiute branch though. The whites kicked hell out of them, and that ended it."

They rode over the pass summit and began the last descent down through a long, sandy, boulder-strewn wash. At the far end below they could see what appeared to be giant dunes of bare sand. Heat now began to strike them with force.

And abruptly, out of nowhere, the Shoshones were there.

Benteen saw them first and halted.

The Shoshones halted too. They were afoot,

and without pack animals, unless you counted the squaws as such. There must have been thirty of them, if you figured the squaws and the kids. Eight braves, if you wanted to call them that, in tattered, cast-off miners' Levi's or overalls, shirts patched with what appeared to be pack rat skins. Their moccasined feet defined them as Indian more than anything else. Unless it was the opaque eyes that stared at the two white men. Eyes that neither Benteen nor Leslie could read.

Benteen's glance noted two pairs of boots instead of moccasins, and he swore.

Leslie said, "They don't look too hostile."

"No? Look again. See those boots? Each pair means some poor prospector was killed to get them."

"They don't look like killers."

"When you're as poor as the Diggers are, you don't have to look the part to be one. You only got to be too hot, or too cold, or too hungry."

"You worried?"

"Notice four of those bucks got rifles. Same source as the boots most likely. And the rest got bows with hunting arrows."

"We'd best parley then," Leslie said.

Benteen held up his hand in a peace sign.

One of the Shoshones stared for a time, then gave a brief return of the gesture. "What you do here?" he said.

"We go down there," Benteen pointed into the valley.

"Too much hot," the Shoshone said. "We just leave."

"We look for white man and white woman. You see?"

The Shoshone leader shook his head.

Benteen pointed to the tracks left in the sand by the mounts of Orozco and Belle.

"No two whites," the Shoshone said. "White woman. Man Messican."

"How far?"

"Not far." The brave looked at him. "You want to catch, you wait. Pretty soon they come back. Too hot down there for Shoshone, too hot down there for Messican and his squaw."

"The Mexican," Benteen said, "he knows the heat."

"Nobody live down there when hot. No Shoshone, no Messican, damn sure no white squaw."

"We go on," Benteen said.

The Shoshone's eyes went to the horses and the weapons of the white men. He smiled suddenly, showing darkened teeth. "You stay with Shoshone. We go up, get nuts, shoot game maybe. Pretty soon the Messican he come back out with the woman."

"We go on," Benteen said again.

The Shoshone's eyes flicked to their boots. He was silent, thinking.

"We pass now," Benteen said.

The Shoshone shrugged. "You damn fool. You come back, one, two day." He smiled his dingy smile again. "We meet then."

"Sure," Benteen said. He kicked his mount and began to edge forward past the halted Shoshones. He kept his eyes on them, even turning his head to do so.

Leslie pulled ahead to lead the way. In a few yards they were partly concealed by boulders. They put the horses into a fast walk until they were out of rifle range.

Leslie blew out his breath. "Thought we might have to shoot our way in," he said.

"May have to shoot our way out," Benteen said. "I've seen sneaky-eyed Apaches aplenty. None sneakier than that chief Shoshone."

"Ain't the kind of man you'd want for a partner," Leslie said.

His words made Benteen scowl. The ex-scout kicked at his horse and pulled ahead of Leslie so that he rode alone.

Leslie wondered if he'd ever find out what it was that was eating Benteen. Whatever it was, it was chewing deep.

It was noon, and the heat on the valley floor was beyond belief. A hundred and thirty degrees Fahrenheit at least, Belle thought. They had traveled all through the night and reached this spot, which seemed known to Sabás, just at dawn.

Now they lay in the shade of mesquite bordering a spring, the furnace air warping all vision around them. She gasped for breath.

Orozco looked pale, but his breathing was easier than hers. And why not? she thought crossly. He was used to the desert, she was not.

His wanness she attributed to his healing wound. He was a tough man, a man who would survive — until that fatal day when the guns of his hunters would shoot him down. He was a badman cast in a heroic mold, she thought. She did not let herself dwell on the things he had probably done. She did not want to spoil the powerful attraction he held for her. She did not understand her feeling at all. She only knew it was there.

At this moment, though, it was somewhat strained.

"I will die here," she said. "Even the water in the canteen is too hot to drink."

"I don't let you die."

"I will die, I tell you! Nothing you can do will stop that."

"We got shade. We got water in the spring. You don't die."

"You goddamn Mexican!" she said. "I'm not like you!"

His handsome face showed hurt.

"Oh God! Sabás, I'm sorry. I didn't mean that."

He smiled faintly. "Is all right, Belle. Is true. A Mexican, he stand heat better. I don't know why."

"I can't breathe."

He gave her a worried look. "Is true, Belle?"

"It's true. This air — my God! It burns your skin to feel it, even in the shade. And we don't even sweat."

"Is because is no water in the air," he said. "One time I hear a gringo prospector say, 'Is no the humidity, is the heat.'"

"How can you joke — when I'm dying?"

"I take you out of here, Belle."

"When? How?"

"We start tonight. We move each night. Rest in day. Three, four days, we get out south end of the valley."

"Four days!"

"We get rid of them hombres that follow that way."

"But they'll die!"

"How can you want that gringo hombre and Sabás too?"

She had no answer for that. Night came and it cooled down to merely hot, and they made fifteen miles by dawn, Orozco told her.

"Two, three more nights."

"And then what?"

"We be back out on the Mojave Desert."

She never would have thought such a destination would be so enticing. Now that desolate expanse sounded like paradise.

She thought of Johnny again. "Are they behind us yet?"

"I see some dust at dawn, I think. Them gringos, they ride by night too."

"So what have you gained?"

"Them hombres, they more smart than I think. No other gringos stay on Orozco's trail like them." He gave her a solemn look. "Your man, he want you back bad."

"The other man," she said, "I don't know what he wants."

"You know him?"

"We have met."

"He is a good friend of your hombre?"

She shook her head. "He is his enemy."

"His enemy? His enemy help him? Why?"

"I don't know," she said. "It is strange." And then she told him what she knew about Benteen, real name Sutter, and why she had been on that stage to Sierra Gorda.

Orozco was thoughtful. Finally he said, "I think he don't kill your hombre until after they catch me. If they catch me, he kill him and get the whole reward."

It was a new thought to her. She said, "But would he hold off on his revenge — just because of the reward?"

"Sure. Gringos, they ain't like a Mexican. They got patience. But don't worry, Belle, they don't catch Orozco."

"If only I could have warned him."

"Too bad for him them Paiutes stop the stage." Orozco let his eyes rest on her sweat- and dust-covered face, still beautiful to him. "Too bad for him," he said softly. "But good for me." He paused. "You want make love, Belle?"

"In this heat? Are you crazy?"

"Goddamn, Belle. You say same thing in that ore bucket."

Leslie and Benteen had adopted the same schedule of chase as that of Orozco. There was no other way. It was impossible to travel during the day. You could not drink the water in the metal canteens during the hours of sun. The water was so hot that it scalded your mouth.

Benteen said, "We're not gaining on them."

"We'll have to keep on in the heat."

"Sure way to die."

"If he gets out of the valley, reaches the open desert, we'll lose him again."

"Well?"

"Like I said, we got to keep on. If we can go part of a day, maybe we'll catch up."

They tried it. Halfway to noon they had to halt. Neither could go farther. Nor could the horses. Only now, where they stopped, there was no spring, no dry bunchgrass for the mounts.

They found a deep arroyo with a high cutbank that at first shielded them from the rising sun, and they huddled there in misery with the horses. But as the sun reached higher, there was no protection from it. They crawled under some greasewood, but that was only slightly better. They sprawled there as first one horse, then the other, collapsed and lay cooking under the broiling sky. And there was nothing they could do to save them. Nothing they could do to save themselves.

The sun slowly passed overhead, and a band of shade began to form on the west side of the dry ravine. They stared at it, trying to muster the strength and the will to crawl to it, wondering if they could rouse the horses to reach it.

Orozco said, "I was think to go out to the south." He was watching her closely as they prepared to move. "But you suffer too much, Belle. I take another way. We go west from the trail a little beyond the springs here. Will take us up into the Panamints where is less hot."

"And then?"

"Is many miles but will take us out halfway between Post Office and Lone Willow. We be back on the desert then."

She nodded weakly. She was almost angry that she felt close to death while Sabás now seemed scarcely bothered by their ordeal. He was getting stronger. The terrible heat, in fact, seemed to have healed his wound.

She made no comment, but he saw the relief in her face. He did not know that part of her relief was because Johnny too might be saved — if he could track them over the new trail.

More and more now, as the hardship of running the Death Valley gauntlet sapped her erotic feelings for Sabás, her thoughts went back to her relationship with Johnny.

The route west began to ascend the foothills. After a few miles it dropped into the wash of a canyon. The low hills on either side were striped here and there with layers of white talc. Miles later they climbed again to a warm-water spring. A couple of thousand feet higher now, the heat was less oppressive.

And near the spring was a crude shelter built of stacked rocks, roofed over somehow with dried mesquite branches.

"Built long time ago by some Shoshone," Orozco said. "Most Shoshone live in brush *jacales*. This Shoshone hombre, he like have comfort."

Comfort was hardly the word, Belle thought.

CHAPTER 14

It was Benteen again who was not fooled by the attempt Orozco had made to mislead his trackers into thinking he had continued south.

They had survived their near-disastrous try to move when the sun was up, and so had the horses. After the long, terrible afternoon in the arroyo, they had ventured out and found a spring five miles farther.

"Now," Leslie said, "what is he up to?"

"I'm guessing Belle couldn't stand any more. He had to get out of that oven or lose her. Maybe he couldn't stand any more himself."

"I doubt that," Leslie said. "He's one tough Mexican. No, he had to do this for her."

"Yeah. I guess a woman like her could make a man do almost anything."

Leslie scowled. When it came to Belle, he never liked Benteen's implications. He said gruffly, "Let's get on with it."

The sight of the rock shelter stopped them. There was some graze around the clearing among the growth of juniper. Behind the hut they could glimpse the pair of horses Orozco had stolen from them, hobbled and grazing but still saddled.

"Must be feeling sure of himself," Leslie said.

"Yeah. Didn't figure we were this close. Well, if they're in there, we got them."

"No shooting. Not with Belle in there."

"Stay here under cover. I'll circle around through those junipers and see if there's a back door to the place." Benteen slipped away.

Nobody stirred that Leslie could see. It made him angry to think of them sleeping side by side in there. Or were they sleeping? By the time Benteen returned, he had worked himself into a state. "Well?"

"No way out. The rear wall is solid rock. We got them trapped for sure."

"What do you mean, 'them' trapped?"

Benteen gave him a sharp look. "Like it or not, they're in there together. Small place — they must be right cosy. You ought to be used to that part of it."

"It ain't easy to get used to."

Benteen grinned slightly. "I reckon not." His grin left him abruptly. "How do you figure to take him?"

"We can't risk Belle."

"That's why I'm asking."

Leslie thought. Finally he said, "Wait him out. He's left the horses saddled, and I noticed the canteens hanging on them. Ready for a getaway just in case. So he's got to come out for water."

"Or send out Belle."

"Think he's seen us?"

"Might have. I was exposed for a piece when I circled out back."

"That could make a difference."

"Wasn't intentional," Benteen said. "Well, there's only one door. He's got to come out sooner or later."

Orozco awoke, knowing something was wrong. He awoke like an animal, all senses alert for danger. From inside the rock hut he studied carefully the approach to the clearing.

Belle was awakened by his movement. She sat up.

"Them hombres, they out there. I see one of them go round back."

She was silent, not sure if she felt this was good or bad. She knew that sometime soon she had to get away from Orozco.

"Goddamn! I sleep too good this time. But I don't expect them hombres. I think they going to follow trail south."

"What are you going to do?"

"I wait till I see that hombre out back come round front again."

"Then what?"

"We go out back way, Belle."

"What back way?"

He smiled. "You see them rocks in back wall? You see, they stacked different. Big hole for take out body, then fill up again."

"What are you talking about?"

"This house, it built by Shoshone. Shoshone believe two things about a house. First, house must be build to face rising sun. Two, they believe when somebody die in house, body got to be taken out fast through opening. Opening that can be closed up quick before spirit of dead can rush back in to haunt house forever. So Shoshone, he build with hole full of loose rock in back wall. So we take out few rock and go. Is why I tie horses in back."

"I'm not going with you."

"You joke with Sabás?"

"I mean it."

His face grew hard. "I been good to you, Belle. Is not true?"

She hesitated only briefly. "Yes."

"You coming with me, Belle. If I got to get mean to make you, I do it."

"I can't stay with you forever."

"Forever? No. Only till I be killed. I told you. It be pretty soon."

"Why do you say that?"

"I always say that. Is going to happen."

"I don't want it to happen!"

"Hell, I don't too. But if you don't want, you come with me. Don't make more trouble for me. I got enough." He was straining now to see as much of the terrain as he could through the doorway without exposing himself. He did not see the conflict of emotions showing on her face.

After a while he said, "I think I see that hombre come back. You and me, Belle, we pick them rocks loose now."

She was sure of one thing at this point. She did not want to see Orozco taken or killed. She dutifully began to help him remove the stacked rocks that hid the Shoshone corpse-removal exit.

Once he had escaped — she was still tussling with that decision.

"He ain't coming out," Benteen said.

"He must have seen you then."

"If he comes out, it'll be shooting."

"He's got Belle in there," Leslie said. "No matter what he does, you be damn sure she don't get hurt."

"That reward money," Benteen said, "it's a sizable amount. If he starts to get away, she'll have to take her chances."

"I'm telling you how it has to be."

"I'm not listening," Benteen said. "What do you think of that?"

Once again Leslie caught the tone of it and wondered. But he was aroused now himself. "She gets hurt, I'll hold you responsible."

"You scare hell out of me," Benteen said sarcastically. He was looking at the rock house doorway. "You ain't talking to a drunk, green kid, like when you were a marshal."

Leslie turned his head to stare at him. "What's that mean?"

"Nothing. I just figure a lot of a marshal's job is manhandling kids out to hooraw a town."

"You have anybody in mind?"

"Ain't that what happened in Jericho?"

"That one time, yeah."

"You say. But I reckon there was others. Man like you, he could build a reputation bigger than he was, just throwing down on hoorawing kids."

Leslie said, "That wasn't my style."

"Been the style of more than one big name."

"Big name? You spent some time in the Territory. You ever hear of me?"

"Never did."

"Well then."

"Drop it," Benteen said. "Right now we got other things to think about."

"Yeah. Wasn't for the horses being hid out back, I'd figure there wasn't anybody in there."

"My way of thinking," Benteen said.

Orozco and Belle had a hole opened wide enough to crawl through.

"You first, Belle."

"No," she said. "You go alone."

"You got to go with me."

"No."

"You going," he said. "Sabás, he been good to you because he want you. But Orozco, he one bad hombre if you make him mad. A bandido. I don't be so much different from Lázaro Nuñez as you think. Don't make me mean with you, Belle."

"What would you do to me?"

He looked at her. There was no expression on his face. But his black eyes had lights in them she had never seen before. "Don't make me do those thing."

She was suddenly afraid of him.

"Go out the hole," he said.

"No!"

The smash of his open palm knocked her down. She was stunned. Then she was crying, crying because he had hit her.

"Go out the hole!"

She crawled toward it. Her head ached from the blow. But that he had done it, that hurt worst of all.

He followed her out. He quickly removed

the hobbles from the horses and replaced the bridles, loosened so the animals had been able to graze. They were still behind the cover of the building. "Mount!" he said, and she did.

He took her reins in his free hand and kicked his heels into his own mount, and they went running.

One single shot was fired behind them. Ahead of them the trail was rough, cluttered with boulders, and as they got among them he reined to a halt and listened.

He and Belle could hear them coming.

"We'll get him soon," Leslie said.

"I'd have got him back there if you hadn't worried about the woman."

Leslie did not bother to answer. He sensed that Benteen said that only to irritate him. For some reason of his own, Benteen seemed to take pleasure in doing that. He was a strange one, Benteen was.

Leslie said, "I been wondering. All the time we been trailing him, he's never taken a shot at us. And he's got our two carbines."

"Makes you wonder about the bastard, don't it?"

"Belle's got some hold on him, I reckon."

"Sure," Benteen said. "She's got goods to trade for him not shooting you." He stared at Leslie and looked pleased as he saw the anger flare again on Leslie's face.

Leslie kept silent. He couldn't argue what Benteen had said. It was just what he himself was thinking.

Benteen said, "Don't it bother you that she don't try to escape him?"

"Maybe she has. Tried, I mean."

"Not too hard, I'm thinking. You may have lost her. Some Mexicans I run into kind of pride themselves as lovers. This one may be that kind."

"I don't want to hear about it."

"Hurts, don't it? Well, Marshal, you better be thinking on it. We get that bastard, you may be some disappointed."

"I said shut up!"

Benteen's face hardened. "You got tall tones for a man needs my help."

Leslie clamped his jaw shut and spurred on ahead.

A carbine cracked, its slug whining off a boulder beside Leslie. Startled, he dropped off his saddle and slipped into cover, tugging his horse with him.

Benteen did likewise. "I guess he's not listening to Belle anymore. Lovers' falling out, maybe."

"Shut up!"

"Tall tones again."

It seemed to Leslie that Benteen was picking

a hell of a time to be growing more disagreeable. Again he wondered about the man's strange moods. One of these days maybe he'd find out what made Benteen tick. That's if a bullet from Orozco didn't finish him first.

It didn't help to think that likely Benteen was right. That Belle had been dispensing favors to protect him, Leslie.

If true, he would be glad if it was no longer so. Even if it meant that Orozco was now out to get him.

That made it even. He was out to get Orozco.

Belle followed only because Orozco still held her reins. That one blow of his hand, so vicious, so unexpected, had changed her feelings for him where nothing else he had done, nothing else she knew about him, had.

It had jolted her far beyond its physical impact. She would never have believed he could do that to her. In one moment of outrage he had destroyed the strange infatuation she had felt for him.

She had never been struck by a man before. Fred Jackson, hardworking and dull, had never come close to physically abusing her. John Leslie — she could not visualize him striking a woman.

But Orozco — he had shown her a side she

should have suspected but had not, caught up as she had been in his romantic allure.

He had said it himself, back there in the Shoshone hut. *Sabás, he been good to you because he want you. But Orozco, he . . . don't be so much different from Lázaro Nuñez as you think.*

She could believe that now. He was bad — he had said so. He was a bandido. She should have expected he could be cruel.

In a single clear moment of vision, she saw what would happen when he tired of her. When their romance wore away under the stress and hardship of his desperate life. She could believe now that he would beat her. Desert her. Possibly leave her to die alone in the desert. She had seen only his good side until now. Now the cracks in his character were beginning to show. Now, for the first time, she was terribly afraid.

CHAPTER 15

A ten-man patrol of the 2nd Platoon, Company I, 1st Cavalry was entering the Panamint Range from the west. It was led by Second Lieutenant Martin Vail. The company commander, Captain Virgil Truett's plan of action called for a string of penetrations into the Panamints in his search for Orozco. Truett himself was at this time up north on the road into the range from Darwin. Between Vail's and Truett's positions several other squads were probing the fringes of the range.

Truett had little hope of finding the bandit. "A hopeless task," he confided to his exec officer. "But we've got our orders."

Lieutenant Vail was no more optimistic as he rode with his troopers up the rugged trail. For guidance he had only a crude map sketched for him by a lone old jackass prospector he had encountered on the Lone Willow Road. According to the map, the trail led up to an area known as Butte Valley.

"Got a butte up there looks like a goddamn tiger," the old man told him. "Fact is, the *californios* used to call it that — Tiger Butte. The damn thing has got vertical stratifications of dark-and-yellow stripes."

"And beyond this Tiger Butte," the lieutenant said. "Does the trail continue?"

"Sure. But you won't be using it. Not in July. It leads into hell, know what I mean?"

"Might Orozco be there?"

"Not likely. Not even him." The prospector seemed hungry for talk. "Hey, you hear what happened down at Lone Willow?"

"I heard the woman with Orozco shot a kid down there," Vail said.

"Well, so it was thought at first. Now the kid ain't so sure. He's healing up all right, and he's beginning to say he thinks it was Orozco himself that done it. Might be it makes the kid feel more important was he shot by the famous bandit, I don't know. Anyhow, he ain't swearing it one way or the other."

"It never seemed likely to me that the woman did it," the lieutenant said, "her being kidnapped by that *cholo*."

"Kind of lean that way myself," the prospector said.

"Well, we'll ride on in to this Tiger Butte you're talking about. That far at least."

"Good luck to you, Lieutenant," the old man said. He continued up the stage road toward Darwin.

The four Shoshones with rifles had been

prowling southward along the higher reaches of the Panamints. They were of the bunch that had confronted Leslie and Benteen earlier in the northern pass. They had set off hopefully to hunt for bighorn sheep but, as they trudged mile after mile and caught no sight of big game, their moods were growing mean.

Most years they managed to get at least a few, usually without going far from their summer rendezvous. It was a ritual of sorts to bag a bighorn or two or three and have a great feast to begin the summer at the higher altitudes.

One of the four was the chief with whom Benteen had spoken, and he was the most frustrated of all. His band would look to him to provide what they had come to expect. If he could not produce, he would lose face.

Already he had been sensing criticism among his followers for not killing the two whites they had stopped at the entrance to Death Valley. He kept thinking about those guns and boots and horses, and he felt in his own heart that he had been stupid. But he had expected the two white men to turn back at the first blast of furnace heat, and he had set up an ambush and waited. They had surprised him and left him feeling the fool.

Never again would he make a mistake like that. Never again would he pass up a chance for quick, easy gain. If he ever sighted those white men again, the guns and boots and horses would be his.

Meanwhile, though, he and his fellow braves were tiring of the hunt for the elusive sheep. Already there were suggestions by his companions that they turn back. It was a long walk back, as it had been a long walk to where they now were. Even if they now found a sheep and killed it, they'd have to pack it on their backs to the rendezvous site. The thought did not improve the chief's disposition.

And when one of the others repeated his suggestion, the chief's temper flared. "We will go on until we can look down on the valley of the striped butte," he said.

Orozco kept looking back at her as he led her mount. At first she avoided his eyes. Then later she met them. She was surprised when he gave her his handsome smile.

"Now I think you be good, Belle," he said. He tossed her reins to her.

She felt she had to say something. "What are your plans?"

"Up ahead is a place called *El Tigre*. I got a idea about that."

"What?"

"I don't tell you, gringa. Because you give

me trouble back there."

"I'm sorry, Sabás."

"You know better now, eh? I make you understand when I slap you, eh?"

She said what she knew he wanted her to say. "Yes."

"Good. We get along like we done before."

She rode along with him as he threaded his way among the strew of boulders. Did he think it was that easy? That she could forget that glimpse of his brutal side? That she could stifle her new awareness of what lay ahead unless she escaped him?

Johnny was behind her. If she could get away and get to him — would he take her back? Would he suspect her willing relationship with Sabás? Even if he did not, would she be "tainted goods" in his eyes?

And there was Sutter back there with him, riding under the assumed name of Benteen, she was sure. If they were together, it meant that Johnny still did not know that Benteen was his enemy. That Benteen was the brother of the Bodie Kid.

She slowly dropped back, hoping Sabás would not notice. For a brief moment, finally, she was far enough behind that she was shielded from Orozco by some rocks.

She wheeled her mount, kicked its flanks, and tried to run.

The horse balked at the boulders in front of it.

And Sabás was directly behind her, and there was rage in his voice. "Gringa *chingada!*" he shouted. "Stop!"

She did not halt. She raked at the horse, but in the confines of the narrow trail it could not move faster. She realized then that she could not get away. But she kept trying.

She could hear him cursing her, and the viciousness of it scared her.

Then ahead the trail widened momentarily and he was instantly beside her, reaching over to grab her reins. In a moment he had pulled up both horses.

"You goddamn gringa whore!" he said.

In her frustration she cried out at him, "Let me go back to him!"

"Never!"

"I can get them off your trail."

"I don't care nothing about that. Up ahead I go to ambush them. *I* get them goddamn gringos off my trail."

"Please, Sabás."

"You ask me please? After you try to leave me? You wait. Up ahead is a place we stop. Sabás, he going to teach his gringa *chingada* a lesson she don't forget." He held up a fist. "With this. You think about that, eh?" He paused. "Some women, they only understand one thing. Sabás he good teacher for that."

"I keep thinking," Leslie said, "about us being after Orozco together. A long way from Jericho for both of us."

"Such things happen," Benteen said. He kept his eyes on the trail through the boulders. He was weighing the odds of being ambushed. He was wondering why Orozco had not tried one yet.

"Where did you learn about the reward?" Leslie said.

"Where did you?"

"From Belle."

"Me too."

"Damn coincidental, ain't it?" Leslie said.

"It is that."

"Don't seem right somehow. Us meeting up and all."

"Pure chance," Benteen said, still not looking at him. "Me being in the bottom of that mine shaft ought to tell you that."

"I guess. Well, like I said before, I'm glad I found you." Leslie paused. "I reckon you feel the same."

"Yeah."

"You don't sound too enthusiastic."

"I got other things on my mind."

They rode a while in silence. Suddenly Leslie said, "I keep seeing that kid's face back there in Jericho. I can't get it out of my head."

Benteen was looking at him now.

"I keep seeing it," Leslie said, "even when I'm looking at you."

Benteen slipped his gun out of his holster.

"What's that for?" Leslie said.

Benteen studied him. "Maybe I'm wondering how close ahead Orozco is."

"You got a slight resemblance to him," Leslie said.

"Who, Orozco?"

"That kid in Jericho."

"A man can't help how he looks," Benteen said. He still held his gun in his hand.

"No, he can't. I guess it's just that I keep seeing his face everywhere I look sometimes."

"That can happen, I guess," Benteen said. "Especially in a man that's got a guilty conscience."

"Why should I feel guilty?"

"I don't know. Do you?"

Leslie was a while in answering. Then he said slowly, "I shouldn't. It was him or me, damn fool that he was." He paused. "I wish you had seen it. Then you'd know."

"Maybe. But maybe I wouldn't have liked what I saw."

Come to think of it, Leslie thought, nobody in Jericho had liked it. Least of all himself.

★ ★ ★

241

From a slope above the valley of the butte, the Shoshones looked down and saw the rider in the *charro* clothes leading by a rope the woman who was lashed, feet tied together beneath her horse, hands tied to the horn of her saddle. They were coming up the trail but were still a ways below the valley.

The chief, thinking back, said in Shoshone, "It was not so before."

"Not so what?" another Shoshone said.

"That the white squaw was bound. Not when they rode into our valley. The white squaw with the Messican."

"I got a squaw like that," the other said. "A woman who won't do what I tell her."

"That Messican, he is one who robs from the mines. A strong warrior. That's why I let him ride in. So he would die from the heat and we would get their clothes later without a fight."

"He was stronger than you thought. He is riding out." The other brave paused. "But we can kill him easy now. And play games with his woman."

The chief nodded. "We will go down," he said.

One of the other braves was figuring in his head. "One pair of boots, two rifles maybe, one handgun, two horses, one white squaw. The best hunting we have yet."

★ ★ ★

Lieutenant Vail said to the squad sergeant, "How far did that prospector say it was to that butte?"

"Ten-fifteen miles of trail, as I remember, sir."

"Can't be much farther then," Vail said. "We've already passed the two springs he mentioned."

"You're right, sir. We must be getting close. Butte striped like a tiger, he said, Lieutenant. That must be something to see."

Vail said, "Don't expect something like the Sphinx of Egypt. People in these godforsaken regions get to seeing things when it comes to rock formations."

"Yes, sir," the sergeant said. "I know that to be a fact."

"I can't figure why he does no shooting," Benteen said. "Unless Belle keeps talking him out of it."

Leslie had been wondering the same thing. For some time now he had been on edge with expectancy, finding increased tension rather than relief as nothing happened.

Adding to his stress was his growing impatience at not being able to get Belle away from her captor. He kept thinking of her as a captive, although he had considerable doubt that this was the true status of her relationship with the *californio* bandit.

And irritating him further was his notice that Benteen was becoming more and more hesitant as he led the way up the rock-strewn canyon.

"For chrissake!" he said. "If you go any slower, you'll stop. We're trying to catch up, not let him get away with her again."

"You ever been ambushed?"

"No."

"I have. When you trail Apaches through country like this, you learn to be careful. If you don't, you're dead. Don't forget, I'm up front here. A bullet comes, I'm the one will take the hit. The trail is plain here. If you're getting itchy, you can take over the lead."

Leslie said, "Move aside then. I'm taking it."

Benteen shrugged. "Go ahead. But there's a saying I heard somewhere, and you might bear it in mind: There are old army scouts and bold army scouts, but there are no old, bold army scouts."

"We ain't tracking Apaches," Leslie said over his shoulder.

"No," Benteen said. "But we're tracking a Mexican who can probably shoot rings around any Injun."

★ ★ ★

Sabás had been in a foul mood ever since Belle's try to escape. She had never seen a man change so much so quickly. She wondered if her action was the sole cause of this, and she decided not. Something else, something greater, was bothering him.

He had been swearing for some time, as he led her, bound, and without otherwise speaking. He swore in two languages, wearing away at her nerves until finally her irritation overcame her newfound fear of him.

"You don't have to keep calling me dirty names," she said.

He stopped cursing and rode in silence for a little while. When he spoke again, his tone was more moderate. "Is not only you, Belle. I got a bad feeling now I don't like. A feeling maybe I die. Maybe you die. If I die, I take both them goddamn gringos with me. They don't going to spend the reward for Orozco."

"You can't blame me for wanting to leave you now."

"Sure, I blame you. I treat you right. I give you *amor* like you don't got since you been a widow. Is true, no?"

Her face reddened from more than the heat.

"And what you do? You run from me when maybe I'm going to die. What the hell woman you are, Belle?"

"I love Johnny," she said.

"You are a gringa *chingada*," he said. "You know the story of *La Chingada*, Belle? She was Mayan woman who was traitor to native Mexican people because she think she love the conquistador Cortez. Ever since, to a Mexican, *chingada* mean a bad word. Now you the same. You traitor to Sabás because you think you love this gringo. So you ready to help him kill me."

"That isn't so! But I *do* love him!"

"Goddamn! You don't know who you love."

"Please, Sabás. Don't ambush him. I'll go away with you. I won't try to get away again."

"Now you beg, eh? But I don't trust you no more, Belle. So you going be tied all the time now."

A couple of miles farther on he halted. He dismounted, dropped his own reins, and went to where she sat dejected in her saddle. He untied the rope that held her ankles.

For a moment she believed he had relented. Then he reached up and dragged her roughly from the horse, tossing her to the ground as he released her. He lashed her legs together and tugged her into cover of the rocks.

He pulled a bandanna from his pocket and gagged her with it, slapping her once on the face as she twisted her head to avoid it. Tears came into her eyes, but he ignored them.

"You don't going to warn your hombre," he said. He stood up and went to the horses and led them a ways up the trail.

A hope came to her, fervent but brief, that John Leslie would reach her before Sabás came back. But it died as he returned within a few minutes.

He grabbed her feet and dragged her into a natural fort of boulders which was slightly higher than the trail.

He had brought back one of the carbines with him. "Now," he said, "we see who kill who. When your hombre come into that clearing down there, you have only one lover left, Belle."

She could not see the clearing he was referring to. She was lying on her back as he had left her, a few feet from him. She could see nothing except the brassy sky. But in her mind she could see what was going to happen.

She could see Johnny, leading the way because he knew she was close ahead of him. Benteen would be behind and would be warned by the first shot fired by Orozco.

That first shot would kill Johnny.

She craned her neck to look at Sabás. He was staring intently down the trail. She heard the strike of hoofs on the flinty terrain. She saw Sabás raise his carbine.

CHAPTER 16

She threw her body into a fast roll toward him. The small rocks beneath her jabbed like dull knives, but she ignored them. She made a complete turn, her face smashing into the ground, before she felt her shoulder strike his legs, knocking him off balance from his crouch. His carbine fired a wild shot into the air as he fell.

He came up swearing and went into another crouch. He looked and saw his target was no longer there.

"I had," he said. "I had your bastard gringo in my sights."

He whirled then and drove the butt of the carbine at her face.

She rolled away instinctively, and he missed. Her back was toward him now, and she waited to feel the smash of the weapon against her skull.

It did not come.

She got herself turned toward him again, and he was looking at her with a strange, mixed expression of rage and horror. There was a sudden sickness in his eyes. He tried to speak and failed.

They looked at each other for a long time.

He said finally, "Oh God! Belle. What I almost done to your face. To your beautiful face!" He got down on his knees then and leaned over and kissed her on the forehead, gently.

She was shocked.

"You make me mad, Belle, is why. I am bad when I get mad." He lifted his head to look down on her. He looked like he was about to cry. "I come close to ruin your beautiful face," he said.

He seemed to remember then about the men on the trail below. He went quickly back to his lookout, then searched appraisingly either side of the shallow canyon. "We got to move. We can't wait here no more."

He came back to her and untied her legs and helped her to her feet. But he left her hands bound and the gag in her mouth, and he kept a grip on her arm. He took her up the trail to where he'd left the horses. He did not take the time to tie her on hers again once she was mounted. But he led once more with the rope.

The Shoshones had come down to the valley and were waiting in the lowest fringe of chaparral. A few hundred feet to the southwest rose the peculiar striped butte that the chief

249

Shoshone knew the *californios* called *El Tigre*. He did not really understand why because he had never seen a tiger.

He waited expectantly as the Messican and his white squaw came nearer, waited for them to get within easy range of the Shoshone rifles. He and his braves were not the best of marksmen — they never had ammunition to waste in practice.

Then to his irritation the Messican turned toward the butte and away from where he and his braves waited. He gave a Shoshone curse, grunted an order, and led them out into the open at a run.

Orozco turned and saw them. He jerked out his carbine and snapped off a shot that dropped one of them in his tracks. The chief shot at him and killed Orozco's horse.

Orozco jumped clear, keeping his grip on his weapon. He fired again, exchanging shots with the chief. Orozco's caught the chief and he went over backward. Blood spurted out of his dirty shirtfront. He was on his back and his heels drummed the ground for a few beats, then stopped.

Belle, with her hands tied behind her, was struggling to free herself from the stirrups as her horse sank to its knees, blood and other liquids running out of it through a hole drilled by the chief's wild bullet.

The two surviving Shoshones ran back into the chaparral.

Orozco let them go as he leaped to snatch Belle free from her falling horse. He drew a knife and slashed loose the lead rope, then tied one end around Belle's waist, the other around his own.

"Come on, gringa," he said, and began to run for the striped butte.

Her first thought was to resist him. She held back against his tugging, trying to dig in her feet. She heard him curse, and then one of the fleeing Shoshones stopped running, turned, and fired a shot that kicked up gravel close to her.

Orozco jerked savagely on the rope, and she stumbled toward him. He shot once at the Shoshone and the Shoshone disappeared into the concealing brush.

Orozco ran again toward the sharp rise of the butte side, and this time Belle ran with him. She had no idea of what were his intentions.

Leslie and Benteen, moving cautiously after the attempted bushwhack, heard the gun battle up ahead, and Leslie increased their pace again. They came to the edge of the valley and stopped to reconnoiter.

They immediately saw the two dead horses

and, nearer to the chaparral, the two dead Shoshones.

"Looks like a couple of those Diggers we saw a few days back," Benteen said.

"Those are our horses," Leslie said.

"Friend Orozco and company were put afoot by the Injuns." Benteen scanned the terrain of the valley.

"Where did they go?"

"He wouldn't try to run on foot," Benteen said. "Without horses, he's got to make a stand."

"On that butte, maybe?"

"Maybe. Curious-looking thing, ain't it? Those yellow-and-gray stripes put me in mind of a sleeping tiger, kind of." Benteen studied the contours of the butte. "That striped side is too smooth to hide them. If he's there, he's off to the right, there where that chasm shows. There's rock there too, and what looks like a depression. He may be forted up there."

"Hell, he ought to know we could wait him out."

"Yeah? For how long? Don't forget Belle is with him. You ready to lay siege until she dies of heat or thirst?"

"Of course not."

"And that'll be just what he's thinking. He'll be figuring we'll have to storm the place

252

to get him. And he'll figure to pick us off when we try."

"Damn smart Mexican."

"That's why he's lasted this long."

"We've got to be careful that Belle don't get hurt."

"He'll think of that too."

They were both silent, thinking about this. Then, abruptly, Benteen said, "All right, gunfighter, how do you figure to take him?"

Leslie looked at the terrain between where they stood and the steep slope of the butte. There were fifty yards of valley floor covered with nothing much except sagebrush and greasewood. The butte side rose then, brush-covered too, with scattered boulders, until it suddenly steepened toward the aerie that Benteen had pointed out a hundred feet above.

It was damn poor cover and concealment, Leslie thought. But there was nothing to do but rush it, leapfrogging, one of them giving covering fire while the other ran, alternating.

He said so to Benteen.

He expected the man to agree and was surprised when Benteen stood staring at him and saying nothing.

"Well?"

"Well what?"

"Are you with me?" Leslie said. "Or do I try it alone?"

"I keep feeling how it was when I was down there alone in the bottom of that shaft," Benteen said. He kept staring at him.

"I wouldn't ask you to repay the favor," Leslie said, "except that it's Belle up there."

"Being obligated to another man is a hell of a thing to be."

"Make up your mind."

"That's harder than you think," Benteen said. It was one way, though, to clear the obligation he owed the gunfighting son of a bitch for saving his life, he thought. If I can once clear that, I can take care of that other obligation, the one I owe to Bert.

And I need his help too to get Orozco, just as he needs mine. Once we get Orozco, and the reward is mine — then is the time to settle the *big* account. Then maybe I can gutshoot the bastard like he did Bert.

"We'll do it your way," Benteen said. "On account of Belle. And the reward of course."

Always the goddamn reward, Leslie thought. All right, you mercenary son of a bitch! He said, "Let's go!"

CHAPTER 17

They lay prone now in the high rocks on the side of Tiger Butte as Leslie and Benteen began their charge.

Belle, her hands still lashed behind her and her ankles again tied, struggled to raise her head to see. The length of rope that tied her to Sabás lay slack between them, but it was still knotted around her waist. He had removed her gag.

"Well, gringa," he said. "Which one you want me to kill first?"

"You mean bastard," Belle said.

"Which one?" Sabás said. "Say it. So I know which one you love." He must have had his carbine sighted ready for one or the other of them, she couldn't tell which.

"Say it!"

The words came frantically from her. "The younger one!"

He fired. "Is dead now, Belle. So now I know the hombre you love. I let him get closer, so I be sure I don't miss." He held his weapon ready to squeeze off another shot.

"Sabás, no! I'll — I'll stay with you!"

"Your hombre, he don't ever give up

chasing me," Sabás said. "So he got to die."
He was intent now on his target.

She threw herself away from him, hoping
to jerk the rope and destroy his aim. There
was too much slack and, too late, she felt herself sliding in loose gravel, unable to stop. She
dropped into a crevice between rocks five feet
below. Her ankle smashed hard and she felt
a bone snap, and she cried out.

Sabás turned his head and swore in Spanish.
He rose to scramble toward the crevice, and
Leslie's carbine sent a bullet ripping into his
chest.

He landed on his side, and blood gushed
from his wound and trickled out of his mouth.
"Ai! Belle! Your hombre he got me through
the lung, I think." His words choked on his
blood. He spat. "Your goddamn gringo, he
kill me, Belle." He coughed. "But I take him
to hell with me."

"No!"

"I kill your goddamn lover now," he said.
He crawled back into firing position.

In the silence of that moment she could hear
his gasping. "Don't kill him!" she cried.

"I see the son of a bitch." His carbine fired.
"Goddamn! I miss."

"Sabás?"

"Belle?"

"If you kill him, I'll die down here. My

256

leg is broken. I can't get out alone."

He did not answer.

"Sabás!"

"I hear." His voice was weak. "I try to think."

"Please! *Please!*"

There was silence. Then his words came, barely audible. "For you, Belle, I do this thing. I go to hell alone."

He must have dropped his carbine then, for it came sliding down into the crevasse and struck her hard on the shoulder. She began to cry then. Not because of her pain, but because of what Sabás had done for her.

She could hear now the sound of John Leslie's boots as he scrambled up the rocky slope toward her.

88371

15